"I will do everything in my power to keep you safe and get your sister back safely," Blake answered.

Liz wanted to believe him. But her natural inclination to keep people at arm's length fought needing to depend on him. But what choice did she have?

It was either go along with his plan or go to jail, which would be a death knell for her sister. Looked like she had only one option.

"Fine." She clenched her jaw. "I'll do it your way."

"Good. You'll have to follow my instructions to the letter if we are to succeed."

Of course he'd say that. He struck her as a man who liked to be in control, to call the shots. "I'll do whatever I have to do to protect my sister."

A wave of fatigue crashed through Liz. Her shoulders drooped. She glanced at her watch. It was after midnight. She hadn't eaten since the midmorning snack on the plane. She needed to find a hotel, but mostly she wanted to get away from this man. "Can I go now?"

Blake rose and picked up the box, tucking the necklace back inside. "I want you where we can protect you."

Terri Reed's romance and romantic suspense novels have appeared on *Publishers Weekly* top twenty-five and Nielsen BookScan's top one hundred lists and have been featured in *USA TODAY*, *Christian Fiction Magazine* and *RT Book Reviews*. Her books have finaled in the Romance Writers of America RITA® Award contest, the National Reader's Choice Award contest and three times in the American Christian Fiction Writers' Carol Award contest. Contact Terri at terrireed.com or PO Box 19555, Portland, OR 97224.

Books by Terri Reed

Love Inspired Suspense

Northern Border Patrol

Danger at the Border
Joint Investigation
Murder Under the Mistletoe
Ransom

Capitol K-9 Unit

Duty Bound Guardian

Protection Specialists

The Innocent Witness
The Secret Heiress
The Doctor's Defender
The Cowboy Target

The McClains

Double Deception
Double Jeopardy
Double Cross
Double Threat Christmas

Visit the Author Profile page at Harlequin.com.

RANSOM

TERRI REED

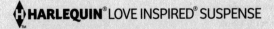

HARLEQUIN® LOVE INSPIRED® SUSPENSE

Recycling programs
for this product may
not exist in your area.

LOVE INSPIRED BOOKS

ISBN-13: 978-0-373-67731-3

Ransom

Copyright © 2016 by Terri Reed

www.Harlequin.com

Printed in U.S.A.

For I know the plans I have for you, declares the Lord,
plans to prosper you and not to harm you,
plans to give you hope and a future.
–Jeremiah 29:11

ONE

A crash from her sister's bedroom brought Liz Cantrell bolt upright on the couch. She was alone in the apartment she shared with her sister and had been seated with her feet tucked beneath her, trying hard to be interested in the movie on the television with no success. She muted the sound and listened.

A floorboard creaked.

No way was that from the blustery January wind outside her second-story apartment.

Someone was definitely in Jillian's room.

Alarm flooded Liz's veins.

"Please, Lord," she whispered as she fumbled to grab her phone from her sweatpants' pocket.

A thud and then a man's deep growl jolted her into action.

No time to call for help. She had to get out of there. Fast. She jumped to her feet and hurried to open the apartment door. The hinge squeaked as loud as a shotgun blast.

Thunder rumbled through the apartment.

Not thunder, but feet. A tall figure, wearing a plastic masquerade mask like those worn at Mardi Gras time and dressed all in black, rushed out of Jillian's room. He had Jillian's big burl-wood jewelry box—thankfully not their mother's special jewelry box—in his gloved hands, spilling the contents of Jillian's costume jewelry on the floor as he ran toward Liz.

Adrenaline fueled her fear. She whirled away and ran for the stairs leading to her family's antique shop, her slippers snagging on the old carpet. The walls of the stairwell seemed to close in on her. She hated dark, confined spaces.

She pushed through her anxiety to scuttle down the stairs as fast as she could. The man came after her, breathing down her neck like a monster from a horror flick, adding to the fear tightening her chest and constricting her throat.

Before she reached the bottom of the staircase, the burglar grabbed a handful of her hair. With a painful jerk, he brought her to a halt and pushed her face-first against the stairwell wall. Pain exploded in her cheek and radiated through her head. Would he kill her? She squeezed her eyes tight, tensing her body in preparation to fight back and sent up an urgent prayer. *God, help me! Help me, please.*

"Where's the necklace?" her attacker growled in her ear. His hot, stale breath made her gag.

"What?" Liz struggled to process what was happening. Why had this man broken into her home? What was he talking about? "What necklace?"

"Come on, Jillian, Travis bragged to me he'd lifted it from Santini's shipment to give to you. Since Travis is so stupid to not keep his mouth shut, he doesn't deserve it. And neither does Santini, the pig." He pressed his weight into her, his knee jamming into her thigh, his elbow crammed into her back at the tender spot below her ribs. "Give it to me or I'll kill you!"

His words beat into her, almost paralyzing her with terror. He thought she was Jillian. What would the man do when he realized she wasn't Jillian but rather her sister? Kill her, then go after Jillian? She couldn't let that happen. She had to protect her little sister.

Stark terror spurred her to action. She

kicked her heel back hard and connected with his shin, eliciting a grunt. She followed with a backward elbow jab to his sternum just as her godfather, the town sheriff, had taught her when she was in high school.

The assailant's hold loosened. She grasped her hair and yanked the clump free from his hand, ignoring the biting pain of strands being ripped from her head. She fled down the remaining stairs into the dark store. He chased after her.

The street lamp outside provided enough light for her to navigate through the antiques filling every square space of the shop her father had bequeathed to her and her sister.

She knocked over a short bookcase filled with rare first editions, hoping to slow her attacker for fear he'd catch her before she could escape.

She made it to the front door and flipped the latch. The door unlocked with a click that was drowned out by her shallow breathing. Opening the door would trigger the silent alarm and send the authorities. With a vicious push, she burst out of the store into the frigid night air, nearly bowling over an older couple walking a big Rottweiler. The dog strained against his leash and barked.

"Help me, please!" She grasped at the older man's arm.

While the couple stood there, mouths agape, she caught a glimpse of the masked man as he barreled out the door onto the sidewalk. He paused for a fraction of a second, his gaze landing on the Rottweiler. He backed up as his gaze jumped to Liz and the elderly couple. With an audible rumble of frustration, he bolted in the opposite direction and disappeared down the darkened street.

A whoosh of relief gushed through her, followed closely by an invading sense of violation. The man had broken into her home and assaulted her. Why was he searching for the mysterious necklace? Neither she nor her sister owned anything of value. He'd said Travis had lifted it—stolen, he meant. Liz had never thought much of Travis from the moment Jillian had brought him home to meet her.

"Oh, my," the gray-haired elderly woman exclaimed. "We should call the police."

The older man patted his pockets. "I don't have my phone with me."

"I do," Liz said just as the jangle of her cell phone in her sweatpants' pocket startled her. With shaky hands, she fished the device out and glanced at the caller ID.

Jillian.

Liz's heart jumped. An icy rush of dread washed over her. After the harrowing experience of the break-in, Liz's imagination took flight with all sorts of horrific scenarios.

She pressed the answer button. "Jillian?"

"Lizzie, I need you to do something for me." Jillian's voice came over the line with a definite quiver.

Every nerve ending in Liz's body alerted, ready to do whatever was needed to help her baby sister. "Are you okay?"

"I need you to bring me Mom's jewelry box. It's tucked into the bottom drawer of my dresser."

"What's going on, Jillian? Some man just broke in—"

"Lizzie, listen to me. I need you to do this." Jillian's sharp tone was so out of character. Pleading, wheedling and coaxing was more her style. Something was definitely wrong.

"Jillian, Travis is mixed—"

Jillian's yelp cut Liz off. The sound of a scuffle on the other end of the line terrified her.

"Jillian!"

"Listen up," a deep male voice said into Liz's ear, sending a shiver of fear down her spine. "If you ever want to see your sister again, alive, you'll bring the necklace to Fort George by noon Monday. Come alone. No police, or your sister and her no-good husband are dead."

Panic revved in her blood. "Who is this? What have you done to my sister?"

The click of the call disconnecting slammed into Liz. Her mind raced. Her first instinct was to dial 911. To seek help from the authorities. Sheriff Ward had always counseled them to come to him if they were ever in trouble. This certainly counted as trouble.

No police, the man had said.

Jillian's life was in danger. Jillian needed Liz to act on the promise Liz had made to their father on his deathbed.

Watch over your little sister, Lizzie, girl, he'd said. *You're the level-headed one. She's going to need you.*

Now more than ever Jillian needed Liz.

Liz dialed Jillian's phone, but it went straight to voice mail. What did that mean? Fear clawed up her throat.

She called the hotel where Jillian and Travis were staying and had the desk clerk ring the honeymoon couple's room, but there was no answer. Liz forced down her panic, knowing if ever there was a time to be calm and clear-headed, it was now.

She refused to think the worst. Not yet anyway. She had a deadline to make. Her sister's life depended on it.

Liz flexed her fingers on the armrests of her seat as the plane dipped with turbulence as it made its approach to her destination. She didn't like flying, in fact, didn't enjoy leaving the island at all. She'd gone off to college at her father's urging, only going as far as Charleston. And that had seemed miles away from the serene island home that Liz loved. She'd returned home for good two years later when Dad had had his heart attack.

But for her sister's sake, Liz was heading north to bring the ransom to free her sister.

Last night, after convincing the sheriff she was okay, she'd spent the rest of the night locked in the downstairs office at the back of the store. She hadn't wanted to take a chance on the intruder returning to find her even though the sheriff had promised a car would patrol the neighborhood.

She'd felt so guilty not confiding to him that Jillian had been kidnapped. But she couldn't risk her sister's life.

Staring out the oval plane window, she could see the white world outside as the plane descended toward the runway in Buffalo, New York. She couldn't appreciate the snowy scenic view with her mind racing ahead with all that she needed to do.

Anxiousness made her antsy as she filed out of the plane and up the jet bridge along with everyone else. The frigid air seeping in from outside made her glad she'd worn her thick fleece-lined down jacket. Still, the chilly air finding its way through the collar of her coat sent a shudder through her. This was a different kind of cold than she was used to. It was biting, like the air had teeth and wanted to sink into her all the way to the bone.

As she exited the jet bridge into the welcome warmth of the terminal, two men stepped into her path. She barely glanced at them before sidestepping, but they followed her move and blocked her exit.

Irritated by the rude behavior, she ground out, "Excuse me."

"Elizabeth Cantrell?"

The deep, smooth voice that hinted at an American Southern drawl stopped her in her tracks. Her attention snapped to the men. How did they know her name?

Both men were tall, broad-shouldered and handsome, yet very different. One had jet-black hair and looked to be of Native American descent. His warm brown eyes regarded her with curiosity. He was dressed in jeans, a warm winter jacket and boots still dusted with snow.

However, the other man's obsidian gaze wasn't warm or curious. He stared at her with such accusation that she took a step back. He wore a wool trench coat buttoned all the way up to the collar and black slacks and black shoes that didn't look nearly warm enough for the weather. His dark brown hair was short and tousled, as if he'd run his fingers through the strands several times. If she weren't so freaked out, she'd have found him handsome, but at the moment all she felt was annoyed and scared and intimidated. A combination that made her body tense.

"I'm Liz Cantrell. What do you want?" She hated that her voice trembled. Were these men sent from the man who had her sister? But how would the man know which plane she was on? A creeping sensation skated over her neck. She was being watched?

The man with curious eyes said softly, "Canada Border Services, ma'am."

What? A panicked flutter started low in her tummy.

"US federal agent," the other said in a low tone. "Come with us."

Neither man wore any identifying logos. Caution told her not to trust them. Wariness crept into her voice. "How do I know you're telling me the truth?"

The federal agent pushed aside his coat just far enough to reveal his gold shield. Then he slid his coat back into place.

A fresh wave of panic washed over her. These men were law enforcement. She couldn't go with them. To do so would jeopardize her sister's life. The man on the phone had told her not to involve the police or he'd kill Jillian and Travis.

She searched for an exit but realized the men had boxed her in. Even if she attempted to run, she wouldn't get very far and would only draw attention to herself. To them. What did they want with her? "Why? I haven't done anything wrong."

The two men shared a glance, then the federal agent stepped to her side and gripped her by the elbow. His big hand was firm but gentle. His woodsy scent surrounded her in such contrast to his cold and accusing demeanor.

"This way, Miss Cantrell," the CBS officer said.

Despite not wanting to attract attention, every instinct in her screamed she shouldn't acquiesce. The man on the phone had told her no police. But these men couldn't know that. And if they knew she had been on this flight, then that meant the kidnapper could also have eyes on her.

"Please, you have to let me go." She dug in her heels but couldn't keep the two men from surreptitiously forcing her to move forward.

"Wait." Her voice rose. She winced. It wouldn't do to show her panic. She collected herself and continued in a hiss, "Where are you taking me?"

They ignored her question and led her away from curious gazes and through a door discreetly situated behind a kiosk. They went down a long hallway. Terror gripped her. Where were they taking her? What would they do with her? To her? What would happen to Jillian? She sent up a silent plea to God for help.

She struggled to free herself but her captors wouldn't let go. The long corridor seemed endless. The tight wall too close. Another door was pushed open, and she was thrust

inside a small room that held a metal table
and two chairs on either side. High in the corner a red light blinked on a camera. She was
in an interrogation room, one like she'd seen
on countless television shows.

A ripple of anxiety coursed through her
veins, making her blood turn to ice. Why
were they detaining her? How long would
this take? What if the man holding her sister hostage found out? What if they took the
ransom?

"We'll be right with you," the CBS officer said before shutting the door and locking
her inside.

The faint smell of antibacterial cleaner
burned her nostrils. She hated to contemplate
the many germs that had contaminated the
room. It wasn't that she was a germophobe
per se. But she couldn't afford to catch a sickness now. Not when her sister's life was in
jeopardy.

Hysteria bubbled up at the ridiculous direction her brain went. A coping mechanism?
The walls closed in on her making her skin
crawl with desperation.

Frantic to escape, she looked for a possible
exit besides the locked door. A window high
in the wall was the only possibility. Pulling

her jacket sleeves over her hands for protection against picking up bacteria or a virus, she tugged at the table but it wouldn't budge. The feet had been bolted to the floor. Using the sleeve of her jacket, she dragged the chair over to the wall below the window and stepped up. Unfortunately, she still couldn't reach the window. So much for escaping. She pounded a fist against the wall, the pain barely registering in her desperate mind.

She jumped down and wedged herself into the corner. Wrapping her arms around her middle, she prayed with everything in her. She'd been entrusted by their father to keep her sister out of trouble. She hadn't done a very good job this time. Thinking back over the many times Liz had had to bail Jillian out of one scrape or another made this latest folly that much worse. Jillian was an adult, but her judgment and maturity hadn't caught up to the number of candles on her last birthday cake.

Dad would be so disappointed. But Liz solemnly vowed to her father's memory that she would do whatever it took to save her sister.

US Immigration and Customs Enforcement agent Blake Fallon watched the woman on the video screen. Elizabeth Cantrell. Or Liz, as she'd been clear to correct him.

Her DMV picture didn't do her justice. Her honey-colored hair draped loosely about her shoulders, and her thick-lashed blue-green eyes reminded him of the Caribbean. The puffy, knee-length jacket hid her figure except for slender, jean-encased legs. The red color of her outerwear highlighted the pink in her cheeks.

His lips had twitched when she'd tried to reach the window. Good for her for at least trying. She was going to need to be brave and brash for what he had planned. He hoped she had the mental and physical mettle to help him bring down an international criminal.

"Here we go," Canada Border Service officer Nathanial Longhorn said as he entered the room.

Blake and Nathanial served together on one of many joint teams consisting of various law enforcement agencies between the United States and Canada called Integrated Border Enhancement Teams—IBETs for short. Other members of their team were working to find the illegal contraband smuggler Idris Santini's far-flung bases of operation in Canada, the United States and Venezuela.

Santini was like a cloud of smoke, visible one moment, then disappearing the next. But now Blake had a viable lead. A way of drawing Santini out into the open where Blake and his team would snag him in a tight net, like the dangerous critter he was. But to do so, Blake would need Liz's cooperation. He'd get it by any means possible.

Nathanial lugged Miss Cantrell's suitcase onto the table next to the video feed and popped open the lid. Nestled inside between Liz's clothing was a small wooden jewelry box. Roses and a hummingbird decorated the lid and sides. It was delicate and appeared old. A family heirloom?

So far Blake's information from his confidential informant inside the Santini organization had proved correct—a woman named Elizabeth Cantrell was planning to bring contraband for Santini into Canada via the border crossing in Buffalo, New York.

Blake snagged the jewelry box and lifted the lid. The rough stone necklace he'd been told about lay at the bottom of the box. He breathed out a relieved breath and untangled the necklace, then stretched it out on the table.

Nathanial snorted. "That's it? Huh. Not what I pictured."

The stones weren't pretty and sparkly like polished, cut diamonds, but were still ill-gotten gains from the blood and sweat of people forced into labor in horrible mining conditions in a developing nation. "These gemstones may not look like much, but each one, when polished and cut, will be worth millions. There's a rumor the head of Venezuela's most violent gang had the necklace fashioned for his wife as an anniversary gift. Santini won't get paid if he doesn't produce the necklace before the date."

Nathanial whistled. "No wonder Santini's so hot to get his hands on it."

"Yes." Acid churned in Blake's gut at the thought of Idris Santini. A man who'd stop at nothing to get what he wanted. Santini and his syndicate of smugglers funded an illegal mining operation in Venezuela. Though the authorities had tried unsuccessfully on numerous occasions to shut down the mine, Santini either bought off or killed anyone who endeavored to thwart him.

A joint effort between the IBETs and the current Venezuelan government had tracked Santini's latest shipment to Miami, then to

Canada. But by the time the IBETs team had the intel, the goods and Santini had disappeared.

Until today. Word was that a single, valuable piece had supposedly been stolen by one of his lower level minions to give as a gift to the man's unwitting fiancée. Blake's informant on the inside stated that Santini had personally abducted not only his man but the man's new wife, Ms. Cantrell's sister, and were holding the couple hostage in exchange for the necklace.

Thus Liz Cantrell was making the trek north.

That the woman hadn't panicked but had followed the kidnapper's instructions spoke to her determination. But not involving the police was pure recklessness. Liz Cantrell was no match for the likes of Santini.

Blake's gut twisted. He hated to think what would happen to Liz and her sister if he didn't intercede.

After swiping the necklace from the table Blake stuffed it back into the jewelry box, then headed into the interrogation room.

Liz had her back propped against the wall, her arms around her torso as if holding herself together. Her gaze lifted from the floor to him. Her pale complexion and frightened eyes tugged at him. He didn't make a habit of intentionally scaring women. But he had to make sure she was malleable so when the time came she'd follow his directions without question. If the need arose her compliance could be the difference between life and death.

Her gaze dropped to the box in his hands. "That's mine." She pushed away from the wall. "You opened my suitcase."

He set the box on the table. "That's what happens when you carry undocumented diamonds."

She made a face. "Diamonds? What are you talking about?"

He narrowed his focus on her. Did she really not know? Or was she playing him? His informant inside Santini's operation said she was an innocent pawn.

Maybe.

Blake rarely trusted anyone. Let alone a man willing to sell out his boss.

Or most women.

In his experience women in general made the best liars and broke their promises much too easily. Truth and fidelity were moving targets, not hard and fast ideals.

But they were ideals that he honored.

He'd let himself be sucked in before by a woman to only be disappointed and hurt when the inevitable happened. He wouldn't make that mistake again. Instead he took to heart his father's motto, *never let your guard down*.

He shook off the memories scratching at his mind. The here and now needed his attention. Santini was the objective. And this woman standing before him was the means to an end. Nothing more.

Blake had pressed his informant for Santini's location, but the man was more afraid of Santini than Blake. It was one thing to report a goods transaction and an entirely different one to give the cops Santini's whereabouts. The informant had bolted, and Blake hadn't heard from him since. But at least Blake had Liz Cantrell. She would lead him to Santini.

Lifting the lid, Blake grasped the diamond necklace, holding it up for her to see. "This."

Her eyes widened. "Those are just rocks."

"No, Miss Cantrell, they aren't." He dropped the necklace. It landed on the table with a clatter. Twelve stones, held together by thin gold wire. "Those are uncut diamonds. Illegally trafficked from the mines of Venezuela."

She shook her head. "No." A hand flew to her throat. "Oh, no." Anger clouded her eyes. "Those aren't mine."

"Are you telling me you're carrying them for a friend?" He tsked and shook his head. "Not the smartest move."

Her lip curled. "You don't understand."

"Try me."

She lifted her chin but remained mute. He had to give her props. She had a spine of steel so far. He didn't know many who'd face him with such bravado, especially women.

He waited, letting the silence draw out. Her expressive eyes revealed her inner turmoil. She was struggling to keep from talking but something held her back.

Was she also more afraid of Santini than Blake?

Picking up the necklace, Blake said, "I'd hate to think you were caught up in something that might land you in jail. Or worse."

She shivered and licked her lips. "May I have some water, please?"

A stall tactic. It wouldn't do her any good to put off telling him what he wanted to know, but he nodded. A moment later, Nathanial brought in a small cup filled with water. Liz drank it down as if she was dying of thirst in a vast desert.

Nathanial left the room.

Deciding to try a different approach, Blake sat, giving her the illusion of authority. "We're here to help you, Ms. Cantrell. All you need to do is trust us."

"I wish I could," she whispered.

Ah, her resolve was weakening. Maybe another little nudge. "If you work with us, then there's less likelihood of going to jail."

"I have to leave," she said with an urgency that sent an alert to his senses.

"What's the rush?" He steepled his hands. "Are you meeting a buyer for the stones?"

Shaking her head, she insisted, "No, it's not like that."

She was close to caving. He would get what he wanted from her. "The only way you get out of here is by cooperating. Tell me what it is like. And tell me the truth."

Rubbing at her temples, she said, "I can't. He said no police. He'll kill my sister."

So his informant was correct. An innocent woman's life was in danger. Now more than ever he needed Liz's assistance. "The only way to get your sister back safely is if you tell me everything."

When she remained stubbornly silent, he reined in his frustration and pushed harder at her with his words. "You see how this is a sticky situation for you?" Blake nodded to the necklace. "You've been caught red-handed with illegal contraband. We could arrest you and put you in jail."

Her eyes grew round with panic. "No, if you do that my sister is dead."

He felt no satisfaction in threatening her. "Then cooperate with me."

A pained expression crossed her face, then she seemed to come to a decision. She squared her shoulders, lifted her chin and met his gaze again, showing her spunk in the way her eyes sparked. "My sister married a man who is mixed up in something bad. Something that neither Jillian nor I have anything to do with. Now she's been kidnapped." She glanced at the stones on the table. "Those are her ransom. If I don't deliver them to—" she frowned but there was no mistaking the unshed tears filling her eyes "—to Fort George by noon tomorrow, he'll kill her."

Anticipation revved in his veins. "Who is he?"

She wiped at an escaped tear. "I don't

know," she ground out. "We didn't exchange pleasantries."

She stepped closer, her pretty face taking on a pleading expression that jabbed at Blake. He fought off the sensation. He couldn't let her get to him. He wouldn't be that weak. His job was his life. And he wouldn't let anything interfere with his job. Especially not a beautiful, gutsy woman, no matter how much respect she stirred in him.

"Please, you have to let me go. My sister's life depends on me giving that stupid necklace back."

"I could charge you with smuggling or even terrorism," Blake stated, gauging her reaction. Her distress appeared sincere. But he had to be sure. He had to know she wasn't involved. That she wasn't lying to him.

Her mouth opened, then snapped shut. She seemed to be reeling in her temper. "I'd never laid eyes on that necklace until last night. Apparently, my sister's new husband gave her the necklace." She slashed the air with her hand. "A man broke into my apartment looking for it. He said Travis stole it from someone named Santini. And now some madman has threatened to kill Jillian if I don't give him the necklace."

"Santini is a madman. A dangerous madman." Deciding he'd pushed enough and needed to proceed with a more gentle manner, he motioned to the chair. "Have a seat, Ms. Cantrell." He purposely softened his tone. "May I call you Liz?"

Slowly, she sank onto the edge of the chair, poised as if she'd bolt at any second. He reluctantly admired her grit. "That's fine."

He studied her for a moment, appreciating the delicate line of her jaw and the high jut of her cheekbones. She was really a striking woman. But not in a made-up or pretentious way. Her attractiveness was natural and came from within her. He'd read the dossier on her and knew she ran an antique store left to her by her deceased father. If this were a different situation, he'd want to know more about her. Did she like antiques? Or was she keeping her father's dream alive at the expense of her own? And what did this woman dream about? Who was she deep down inside?

A fighter. He knew that for certain.

Shaking off the uncharacteristic musing, he said, "I'm Blake. Agent Blake Fallon with

Immigration and Customs Enforcement. It's my job to help secure the northern border of our country from illegal activities. Activities that Santini engages freely in. Do you understand?"

"Of course. I'm a law abiding citizen. Normally, I wouldn't… I have never broken the law."

Appreciating her attempt at defending herself, he kept his tone soft as he said, "Liz, I do want to help you."

She scrunched up her nose in obvious confusion. He was momentarily distracted by the cute motion.

"You'll help me?" she asked. "How?"

He took no triumph in having her right where he wanted her. If they were going to see this through, he needed her to be willing to do what he asked of her. "You'll need to help me, too."

Her eyes narrowed in wariness. "What do I have to do?"

Valuing her caution, he placed his palms on the table to keep from curling his fingers into fists. The burn of anger at Santini simmered below the surface, ready to boil any moment. "Help me bring down Idris Santini."

A little V appeared between her eyebrows. "Who *is* this Santini character?"

Blake's fingers dug into the table. "A very bad man. He killed a fellow ICE agent in cold blood."

Sympathy flooded her eyes. Blake tried to look away but couldn't. Her gaze pulled him in, made him want to make her understand the magnitude of the situation. "Our intel had put him at the docks in New Jersey. Liam and I were the closest agents. I was in Manhattan, and Liam was in Atlantic City. Liam arrived first and, without back up, tried to prevent Santini from boarding a freighter. When I arrived Santini had Liam on his knees. I watched the man put a bullet in the back of Liam's head and toss him off the side of the pier like garbage." Blake's fingers curled into tight fists. "Liam should have waited for me."

"Would you have waited for him?"

The question so quietly asked had the power of a chainsaw and ripped through him, forcing him to confront a truth he hadn't wanted to face. "No. I would have done the same."

"And then you'd be the one dead."

Acid burned in his gut. He wanted to believe he wouldn't have let Santini get the drop on him. But Liam was the best there was. "It shouldn't have happened."

"I'm sorry for your loss," she said, her voice gentle.

He leaned forward. "And now Santini is threatening the life of your sister and her husband. We need to work together to bring him to justice and rescue your sister."

Blake vowed to take Santini down if it was the last thing he did. And this woman was the key to Blake's revenge and redemption. He just needed her cooperation.

"Why should I trust you?" Liz asked with skepticism lacing each word.

Blake stared her in the eye and flattened his hands on the table. "You have no choice if you want to see your sister again. In order for us to succeed, we have to trust each other."

TWO

No choice.

Staring at the man across the metal table in the interrogation room, Liz clenched her jaw until her teeth ached.

ICE agent Blake Fallon.

He took the acronym to a whole new level. She didn't doubt ice ran in his veins. Waves of tension rolled off him, adding to her own anxiety. And yet he watched her with measured patience as if he had all the time in the world. There wasn't an extra ounce of fat to him, no softness whatsoever. His lean frame and wide shoulders blocked her view of not only the door but also the exit. He had a strong jawline, defined cheekbones and eyes so dark she could see her reflection.

Could he see how terrified she was? Did he even care? She knew that wasn't fair. His story of his friend's death left an impression.

He blamed himself for something that was out of his control. Most likely he thought he could have prevented the tragedy. She had a feeling control was important to him.

And he wanted her to trust him because he said so.

Well, that wasn't how trust worked. He had to prove himself trustworthy if he wanted her to believe that he could help her. Because from where she was sitting, it appeared as if he wanted to intimidate her into doing whatever he wanted her to do. To bring down Santini. A man who had murdered his friend. And now held her sister captive.

Under normal circumstances, if a man had acted so domineering she'd be out the door and on her way without a backward glance.

But these weren't normal circumstances.

And Agent Blake Fallon wasn't just any man. He was the man who held the power to free her sister.

Did he know about the other man who had threatened to kill Liz if she didn't hand over the necklace?

Jillian's new, no-good, rotten husband had put Jillian and Liz in danger, not to mention himself. Poor Jillian. Liz prayed she wasn't too heartbroken to learn Travis wasn't the man she'd thought him to be. Unfortunately, he *was* the kind of man Liz feared he'd be. Calculated, conniving, a thief.

She blew out an angry breath and forced back the fear that lurked at the edges of her mind. She had to be sensible and think this all through.

One mistake could cost Jillian her life. That wasn't a risk Liz was willing to take. She grew hot beneath her jacket. She unzipped it and let the sides flop open to allow for the mild air of the interrogation room to swirl over her, cooling her thoughts as well as her overheated body.

"You didn't answer me," she intoned with a good measure of annoyance she couldn't hold back. "What do you want me to do?"

He arched one dark eyebrow.

She grimaced. "Besides trust you, that is."

For a second amusement danced in his eyes, and she thought he might smile. But no. Just as quickly his stoic expression slid back into place, making the angles and planes of his face hard and unyielding. It must have been her wishful thinking that the man had some other mode besides stony.

"We both want the same thing," he said in a slow measured tone. "Santini."

She sat up straighter. "I want my sister back. Unharmed."

Those were two different agendas.

He inclined his head, acknowledging her words. "That's a given and obviously my priority. But until we bring down Santini, there's no guarantee you'll get your sister back. Unharmed."

His response made her stomach clench with apprehension. She wanted to deny the truth in his words. But judging by where she was sitting and who was glaring at her across a cold, hard table, she figured he probably knew more about Santini and situations like this than she did. But that didn't mean she had to like it. Or him.

"He told me no police or he'd kill her," she pointed out.

"Let me worry about that."

Right. Like that was going to happen. "You still haven't told me what I need to do."

"You'll make the drop like Santini demanded. Only we'll have people everywhere. When Santini shows up to pick up the necklace, we'll nab him."

"That's your plan?" she asked. The man appeared intelligent, but maybe he had rocks for brains. Great. Not inspiring a lot of trust right now. "I don't think this Santini guy is going to be dumb enough to walk into a trap. At the very least he'll send someone to make the pickup."

"You're right, he's not dumb." Blake's fingers stretched against the scarred metal table. His jaw hardened. "He's a smart, crafty criminal. But he's also greedy. Do you have any idea how much that necklace is worth?"

"No."

Again he raised an eyebrow. "Let's just say your travel insurance wouldn't have covered it if your luggage had been lost."

She swallowed. "How much money?"

"To give you an idea of their potential worth, recently a vivid blue diamond sold for twenty-four million."

The staggering amount left her breathless. "That necklace has two…"

"Exactly. Santini won't risk letting another minion snatch it out from under him again. He has a buyer standing by. There's a lot of money at stake. I know Santini. He's greedy and arrogant. He'll come for it himself." He held her gaze, his dark eyes compelling and unfathomable. She grew uncomfortable beneath that stare, yet she couldn't look away.

"And he doesn't know we have you. Nor will he know you're working with us."

Blake sounded so confident. But she wasn't convinced. She needed him to assure her because he was asking her to place her life and her sister's life in his care. He said Jillian's release was his priority. Was that true or just lip service to get her to acquiesce to his plans? "How can you be sure Santini doesn't have spies in your department? On your team? Men following me? You say you've been after him but unable to catch him. Have you ever considered the reason might be someone in your organization is working with Santini?"

Blake's eyes narrowed. "Believe me I've thought of every possibility. I've had everyone involved in Santini's case carefully vetted. This IBETs operation is small for a reason. I've handpicked each member. There is no way any one of them would betray the team."

She wanted to believe him. There was something in his tone that spoke of his determination and frustration. Despite his best effort to control the circumstances, he couldn't. Santini somehow managed to evade capture time and again. And for a man like ICE agent Blake Fallon that had to be driving him mad.

"Do you know who the man was that broke into my apartment last night?"

"No. Unfortunately, he wasn't on our radar until after we found out about him attacking you." He didn't sound pleased. "Now that we know he's involved and on the trail of the necklace, we'll be on the lookout for him. Did you get a good look at him?

"No. He wore a mask and it was dark. Don't you know what he looks like? How is he connected to Travis? To Jillian?" She shuddered, remembering the vile man's voice and the way he'd grabbed her. She thought for certain he would hurt her. "He threatened to kill me, thinking I was Jillian."

"The best we can surmise is this man wants to usurp Santini's throne. My informant gave me a name, Ken Odin, but we can't find him in any databases."

The thought that there were two men out there that wanted to do her and Jillian harm had her pulse picking up speed. She clasped her hands together to keep them from shaking. "He claimed Travis bragged about stealing the necklace from Santini."

"I doubt Travis understood the magnitude of what he'd taken from his boss. If he'd had any idea the value of the necklace or the trouble that would come down on his head, I doubt he'd have stolen it. Unless he really is that reckless." Blake steepled his hands. "But because he did steal it we have an opportunity to use the situation to our advantage."

Which brought them back to the plan where Blake hoped to lure Santini out into the open and capture him. "So I go to Fort George with the necklace to wait for Santini."

Blake gave a short nod. "Yes."

She'd never done anything dangerous before. She'd lived her life following the rules, making sure everyone had what they needed and picking up the slack where she could. Putting herself deliberately in harm's way went against her own sense of self-preservation. But for Jillian she had to. And she had to rely on this man to protect her. "And you'll be close by watching, right?"

His expression softened slightly. "Yes."

The small glimpse of consideration, of compassion, didn't assure her, instead it made her heart beat too fast and her mouth turn to cotton. It was clear he knew what he was asking of her was dangerous and yet, he still asked. And she had no choice but to confront her fears and do what needed to be done. For her sister's sake. And for her own. She wouldn't be able to live with herself if she hadn't done all she could to rescue her sister. She swallowed, trying to find her voice again. "If I don't cooperate with you, I'll be arrested." The thought of jail terrified her. She didn't want to go to prison. If she were incarcerated, who would save her sister? "Is that, right?"

"Yes." His frown wasn't a scowl but more troubled, which made her wonder if he wasn't as happy at the prospect as she'd have thought.

Maybe he wasn't as cold as he'd like her to believe. But then again, he was asking her to risk her life by following his plan. Was she crazy to trust him? Did she trust him? She smoothed her hand over her denim-clad thighs. "What happens if he doesn't bring my sister to the fort?"

He didn't flinch. His expression hardened. She hadn't thought it possible. His jaw must ache with tension. "When we have him in custody, we'll get her whereabouts from him."

A sour taste settled on her tongue. That wasn't very reassuring. "What if Santini doesn't show up?"

"Then we'll follow whoever does take the necklace." His words held a thread of impatience that hadn't been there before. Was he not used to anyone questioning him? "They will lead us to Santini."

"And to my sister," she reminded him with a good dose of her own hardness infusing her voice.

He nodded and visibly seemed to check himself. The impatience dissipated to be replaced with a placating look that grated on her nerves. "We have every intention of recovering your sister."

His words should have assured her even if his expression infuriated her, but the way he said *recover* made her think the worst. A chill scraped across her flesh. The cold, harsh room seemed to close in on her, stirring up old fears to mingle with new ones. How had her life come to this? What should she do? How did she save her sister?

Please, Lord, don't let anything bad happen to Jillian. Give me wisdom. And the courage to act. "What will happen to her husband, Travis?"

"He'll be arrested along with Santini's other men."

Jillian would be devastated. Liz would help her through her disappointment, and they would go home together to resume their lives, hopefully putting this whole ordeal behind them.

"What if Santini figures out you're there?" A shudder rippled through her as possible scenarios played through her mind. She'd be an easy target if Santini decided to eliminate her. And her sister. "Can you guarantee my safety? My sister's safety?"

"I will do everything in my power to keep you safe and get your sister back safely," Blake answered, his voice low, resolute.

His determination rang through. He believed what he said, but could she? Could she put her life in his hands? Did she have faith enough to rely on someone else? Her natural inclination to keep people at arm's length fought her need to depend on him. Depending on anyone was such a foreign concept. Did she have it in her to do so? What choice did she have?

It was either go along with his plan or go to jail, which would be a death knell for her sister. It looked as if she had only one option. A hard option for her. It would require her to dig deep to find the necessary will to trust, to count on this man.

"Fine." She clenched her jaw, mirroring the way he'd gritted his teeth earlier. The accom-

panying ache had her pressing her lips together to relieve the pressure before saying,
"I'll do it your way."

A flash of relief crossed his handsome face.
Had he really thought she wouldn't cooperate,
given he'd threatened to arrest her?

"Good." His tone wasn't nearly as sharp as
it had been before. "You'll have to follow my
instructions to the letter if we are to succeed."

Of course he'd say that. His words confirmed her assessment that he was a man who
liked to be in control, to call the shots. Well,
she had a dose of that, as well. She arched an
eyebrow. "I'll do whatever I have to in order
to protect my sister."

"I wouldn't expect anything less."

His voice vibrated with respect. The odd
turnaround had her mind spinning. He approved of her standing up to him? For some
reason that pleased her and irritated her at the
same time. Had he been baiting her to see if
she'd fold under the pressure?

She hadn't. At least, not yet. She was too
worried for her sister's well-being. When this
was over and they were both safe, then she'd
collapse. But not in front of Blake Fallon.
That would be not only humiliating and de-
grading, it would let him know that her bra-

vado was just that—bravado, manufactured and fragile. But she would be brave. She had to prove to Blake, to herself, that she had the mettle to see this ordeal through. Only with God's help could she do it.

A wave of fatigue crashed through her. Her shoulders drooped. She glanced at her watch. They'd been here for a long time. She hadn't eaten since the midmorning snack on the plane. She needed to find a hotel, but mostly she wanted to get away from this confusing man. "Can I go now?"

Blake rose and picked up the box, tucking the necklace back inside. "I'll escort you to a safe house."

Oh, goodie. Not. She would rather go alone. Then she wouldn't have these confusing and conflicting thoughts about the agent. "I'll find a hotel, thank you."

"Not happening." His tone was adamant. "I want you where we can protect you."

Despite how irritating she found him, she couldn't deny that having some protection eased some of her anxiety. She'd be stupid not to accept. She'd already agreed to his plan, she now had to find it within herself to allow him to protect her in every way. That included her accommodations.

"Fine. You can be in charge of where I stay." She rose and held out her hand. "My box, please."

She wasn't going to let the box or the necklace out of her sight. The necklace was her only bargaining chip and the box's sentimental value was worth more to Liz than the price of the uncut diamonds.

He hesitated for a moment, clearly uncomfortable letting her take ownership of the priceless bauble, before placing her mother's jewelry box on her palm. Her fingers closed around the wood, feeling the carvings dig into her flesh. Liz traced a finger over the roses carved into the side. A wave of sadness washed through her as she held the box in her shaking hands. She missed her mother so much. Liz had been only ten when she'd passed, but her memories of her mother were still very vivid and bolstered her courage.

Liz was going to need every ounce of strength she possessed to make it through this nightmare. She sent up another silent prayer for help and safety for Jillian, for herself, as she followed Blake out of the interrogation room.

The CBS officer waited for them in the hallway with her suitcase. "Exit through that door." He pointed to the opposite end of the hallway from where they'd entered.

"It needs to appear that you're going about the plan as normal, so go straight to the rental car pickup," Blake told her. "There's a phone in the glove box of your rental. When it rings put it on speaker so I can give you directions. I'll be right behind you."

Apparently they had anticipated her cooperation. She should be angry, but she was too freaked out and tired to stir the embers of anger. Though she nearly let loose a hysterical chuckle, no doubt born of fatigue and panic. Blake was certainly sure of himself. That could be a good thing. At least she hoped so. She grabbed the handle of her luggage and rushed out the exit, which led her back to the terminal.

She hurried through the security exit and out of the airport. Stars twinkled in the dark sky. She took a moment to breathe in the cold air to clear her head. The freezing temperature was painful to her lungs. Within seconds her face felt as if icicles were forming on her skin.

She crossed the street, heading to the car rental desk and stepped into line. A large body bumped into her, knocking her off balance. "Hey!"

A hard object pressed into her side. "Don't scream or I'll put a bullet in you."

Terrified, Liz stiffened. She recognized the voice whispering in her ear. It was the intruder from her apartment. Santini's rival for the diamond necklace. She turned her head, wanting to see his face.

But he shifted out of her peripheral view and pressed the barrel of the gun harder into her ribs and growled, "Don't look at me. Just walk."

Frantically, she searched for Blake as she stepped out of line with the man and moved toward a waiting car. She couldn't make out the driver's face. His dark gray hoodie covered his head and hung over his face.

The blare of a horn caught her assailant's attention.

Liz's gaze whipped to the left in time to see Blake jump out of a nondescript sedan and run full speed toward her. From the corner of her eye she saw the Canadian customs officer racing to intercept her attacker.

The man with the gun cursed, then pushed her away, sending her stumbling toward Blake. Her would-be captor jumped into the waiting vehicle before the customs officer could reach him, and the little blue coupe took off like a rocket, weaving through traffic. The customs officer was on his phone in seconds, presumably calling other law enforcement to pursue the two men.

Blake grabbed her by the biceps. "Are you okay, miss?"

Taking his cue to act as if they didn't know each other, she nodded, "I'm fine, thank you."

She shrugged out of his hold, unsettled by the way his hands burned through the material of her coat to her skin.

He nodded and returned to his sedan. His tall, lean frame folded into the driver's seat. She watched him drive away with anxiety twisting her up in knots. Feeling exposed, she hurried to the car rental counter. After signing for the rental car, the man handed her a set of keys to a silver sedan.

Once inside the vehicle, she locked the doors and then opened the glove box to find the phone Blake had said would be there. She had to admit she was grateful to have him on her side. She was nuts to think she could have pulled off rescuing her sister alone. Within seconds the small cell phone rang.

She pressed answer and then the speaker button as she'd been instructed. "Hello."

"All right, Liz," came Blake's voice. Some of her tension eased, knowing she had a link to him through the phone. "The address where you're going has already been programmed into the car's onboard GPS. Start the car and hit the route button. I'll fall in behind you. Nathanial will also be following. If we think you're being followed, we'll give you further instructions."

"Okay." Her hands shook as she started the car, then hit the route button on the navigation system in the dashboard. Immediately a disembodied female voice gave her directions to follow.

She gripped the steering wheel tightly as she drove through traffic. A surreal sensation blunted the edges of her fear. Was she really doing this? "That man with the gun was probably Ken. He was the same man who broke into my apartment. I recognized his voice."

"I'll let Nathanial know."

A shudder worked through her, tensing her shoulders even more until they were hiked all the way to her ears. The man had almost had her for a second time. Thankfully, Blake had been there. But could she count on him to save her again? To save her sister?

She prayed so. Because if Blake failed her, then her sister would die.

"Nathanial caught the license plate of the vehicle he jumped into." Blake's voice filled the car. "Local police will track it down, but I'm sure those two will ditch it and find other transportation."

"He must have been on my plane," she said, realizing that if Blake hadn't detained her, that man might have succeeded in kidnapping her and taking ownership of the necklace.

"He used an alias," Blake told her. "We'll have our people reexamine the flight manifest and see if we can catch him on any of the airport's video feed."

"The other guy must be local and provided him with the gun," she hypothesized.

"Yes, that thought crossed my mind," Blake admitted.

She sighed. "I'm freaking out that there are two people trying to claim the necklace as theirs."

"It does complicate things but don't worry, we'll keep you safe."

She hoped so. "I appreciate that."

Traffic slowed as she approached the Rainbow Bridge where she'd cross the border over the Niagara River. She glanced in her rear-view mirror and realized Blake was in the car directly behind her. For some reason that made her feel protected and exposed at the same time.

She crossed into Canada without incident and continued to follow the navigation system to a tall red brick building.

"Circle the block," Blake instructed. "To make sure no one is following."

She did as he asked, noting that he'd fallen back by several cars. When she passed the front of the building the second time he said, "We're clear. Park in the garage and wait in the car for me."

She found a parking spot in the corner near the stairs. A few minutes later, Blake drove in and parked two places down.

He hopped out of his car and walked over to her. She unlocked the doors so he could grab her bag from the backseat. She climbed out and came around to his side.

"This way." He led her up the stairwell and into the building's entryway. Warmth suffused her, chasing away her chill. She shrugged out of her coat and draped it over her arm as she looked around. Immediately she was taken with the marble floors, the art deco decor and the lovely antique pieces scattered around the lobby.

"What is this place?" she asked.

"Where the team is staying," he answered.

The ding of the elevator car arriving echoed off the polished marble floor and cut her off from asking more questions about her surroundings. The doors slid open. Staring into the box, her throat constricted. The muscles in her shoulders tensed. He laid his hand to the small of her back, urging her to move. His touch was warm through her pink sweater and created tingles on her skin, distracting her enough to enter the elevator car. She plastered herself against the wall and gripped the handrail as Blake entered, dragging her suitcase behind him. He was a good head taller than she and so attractive he stole her breath.

The doors slid shut, trapping her inside the small car with Blake. He took up too much of the oxygen. A light-headed sensation had her bracing a hand on the gleaming metal wall. He gave her a curious glance but made no remark.

She chalked her dizziness up to a bout of claustrophobia or lack of food. Either could be the culprit, certainly not because of the good-looking agent.

They got out on the eleventh floor, and he led her to a door at the end of the hall which he unlocked and pushed open. "Inside, please."

Curious, she entered, thankful for the soft yellow glow from a table lamp. The large living room held two brown leather sofas and a love seat, a glass coffee table, a marble fireplace, plus a plush rug that cushioned every step. She laid her coat over the arm of a high-back chair pushed up to a nice-sized dining table. Off to the right was a kitchen. Without the lights on, she couldn't make out more than the shapes of the appliances, but would hazard a guess it was all state-of-the-art.

Blake walked past her and down a short hall. "This will be your room."

She followed him into a well-appointed bedroom with crisp white linens, a marble fireplace and floor-to-ceiling windows that during the day would offer stunning views.

The room faced the falls. Though it was too dark to see the water, she could make out the slight hum of the rapids. There was a thin television mounted on the wall over a desk. The bath was equally impressive. Oversized with marble accoutrements and gold fixtures. Bright white plush towels hung on warming racks and a thick white robe waited on a hanger on the back of the door.

As much as Liz appreciated the luxury of the condo, she'd rather be home with her sister, both of them safe and content to be on Hilton Head Island.

"I shouldn't be here," she said. Guilt ate at her. She was in this beautiful place, protected and safe, while who knew what kind of conditions Jillian was suffering. "I should be at the hotel where Jillian last was. Maybe there's a clue or something that will tell us what happened to her."

In two long strides Blake was in front her, towering over her, yet she didn't cower. His posture was unthreatening, almost tender. His big hands engulfed her much smaller ones. His touch was comforting and disconcerting all at once. She saw the shadow of fatigue under his eyes and the stubble darkening his strong jaw. He still had his coat buttoned to the top and looked as if he'd stepped from the pages of a magazine rather than being an agent for the federal government.

She should pull her hands away, the rational part of her brain warned, but she didn't.

Couldn't. For the moment, she accepted his offer of strength.

"Listen to me, Liz, you're going to need to be alert and one hundred percent ready for tomorrow. That means rest for the remainder of the night."

Easy for him to say. "I don't know if I can rest."

"You need to try." He rubbed her hands gently. "We have people staking out the hotel. If your sister returns, they'll let me know."

Her stomach cramped with hunger. "Would it be possible to get a piece of toast and a glass of water?"

"Of course. I'm sorry, I should have offered the moment we arrived." He ran a hand through his hair. "I'm not used to playing host."

She tracked his fingers, wondering if the dark strands would be coarse or soft against her own skin. Forcing her attention away from his hair, she said, "It's okay. You've a lot on your mind."

"This way." He gestured for her to follow him.

He unbuttoned his coat as they went, then shrugged out of it and laid it on the back of the couch. The suit he wore looked to be perfectly made for his physique. The navy material draped on his frame in a custom fit that emphasized the width of his shoulders, his trim waist and long muscular legs.

"When did you last eat?"

It took a moment for his words to process. She had to drag her mind away from admiring him. "This morning," she admitted.

He turned the kitchen light on. She was right. Gleaming, state-of-the-art, appliances and granite countertops. She traced her hand over the cool surface. Her apartment counters were old white tile blocks that needed regrouting.

Blake leaned on the open refrigerator door. "I could make you some eggs or a salad."

"Eating too much this late at night will give me the gobbly-wobbles." Not as if the past twenty-four hours hadn't already. She would no doubt have nightmares tonight. That was if she managed to sleep at all.

"Uh?"

She smiled with sadness. "Sorry. That's something my dad used to say. Add to my nightmares," she clarified. "Toast will be fine."

He frowned at her. "You have nightmares?"

"Not on a regular basis but my sister has been kidnapped. What do you think?"

"Oh, right." He reached inside the refrigerator and brought out two loaves of bread. "We have sourdough or cinnamon raisin."

Her mouth watered. "One of each."

"All right," he said with a dose of approval that shouldn't have felt so good. "One of each it is. Glasses are in the cupboard to the right of the sink." He popped two slices of bread in the toaster.

She got herself and him tall glasses of water. When the toast was ready and buttered on a plate, they sat at the dining table while she nibbled on the toast.

Blake leaned back in his chair. The dropdown light over the dining table covered him in a soft glow, gentling the sharp edges of the angles and planes of his face. "Tell me about your family's business."

Was he really interested or making small talk? It was hard to tell from the neutral expression on his face. Deciding it didn't matter either way, she replied, "My dad was a professor of history when he met my mother. She'd worked in a coffee shop near campus. They had a whirlwind romance that lasted two decades. Mom loved antiques so buying the store on Hilton Head Island gave them a common interest."

"So they ran the store together?"

"They did, until mom's illness. Lymphoma."

"I'm sorry for your loss." He sounded sincere, and she appreciated his consideration.

"Thank you." She finished off her toast as a wave of exhaustion took hold. "Dad was never the same after she passed. Ten years later his heart gave out. But I think he died of a broken heart."

"Leaving you to care for your younger sister," Blake said.

"Yes. I promised my dad on his deathbed I would take care of Jillian." From the moment her father had elicited the promise to watch out for Jillian, Liz had been doing so. She'd come home from college to finish out her last two terms via online classes and worked in their father's shop while Jillian finished up high school.

"You were what, twenty? Surely you had other family who could take some of the burden?"

"Both my mom's and dad's parents passed on when we were little. It was just me and Jillian."

"What is she like?"

"Pretty like our mother. She got Mom's fine bones and masses of curly blond hair. A free-spirited artist." But Liz had the more angular features of their father and her dishwater blond hair was stick straight. No matter what type of styling equipment she used, she couldn't get her fine, thin hair to curl. "I take more after Dad."

There were other differences, as well. Jillian was also reckless, always chasing after one dream or another, while Liz analyzed and contemplated before making any decision. Over the years Liz had endeavored to curb her sister's wild ways to no avail.

"Was he reserved and thoughtful, like you?"

She'd been called reserved often. She didn't mind that moniker. Opening herself up to others didn't come naturally or easy. But Blake considered her thoughtful? That was nice. He was nice when he wasn't trying to intimidate her.

"Dad was passionate about the store. So in that respect, yes, I'm like him. I enjoy running the business. Over the years Dad taught me how to manage the inventory and the books so when he passed on it was a given that I'd take over while Jillian finished high school and then dabbled at college."

Anxious dread weighed down her heart as worry bubbled. Was Jillian all right? Was she resting? Getting food to eat?

"Yet you managed to finish college," he said sounding impressed.

"I did." She was proud of the accomplishment. "My degree in marketing has proven effective with the store."

"So you run the shop and provide for Jillian." He cocked his head to the side. "Who watches out for you and your needs?"

His question caught her off guard. She had no ready answer. She'd been content to manage the store while Jillian went off to college to study art. Her passion, as Jillian had claimed with dramatic flair when Liz had suggested she major in something a bit more practical.

She didn't regret the time spent keeping the business going or providing as much guidance as she could for Jillian. It was her choice to honor her father's promise. And she would continue to do so. Jillian needed her now more than ever.

Deep inside of her, resentment stirred for the promise she'd made, the years of sacrifice.

And as quickly, guilt swamped her, flooding her heart and her mind, drowning the resentment. How could she not want to keep her promise to her father? How could she begrudge taking care of her sister?

Still Blake's question poked at her, forcing her to admit to herself that the last time she'd felt cared for had been before her mother had fallen ill. A heavy sadness pressed on her shoulders. Mom had been so loving and kind, yet she'd been stern when needed. She'd been encouraging and giving. Liz had admired her so much. And had wanted to emulate her in every way. When the sickness had grabbed ahold of her, Liz had stepped up to fill her shoes by taking over the household chores and the cooking and even taking care of young Jillian.

Dad had tried to stay involved in their lives, but he'd been so consumed by his wife's illness that the day-to-day living had fallen to Liz. She'd picked up the mantle with pride. Still did.

"I'm doing fine. It's Jillian who we need to be worried about." She picked up their dirty dishes and carried them to the sink, hoping he'd drop this line of conversation. She could feel his gaze on her but she held her chin up and wouldn't let him see how his question affected her.

"We have a big day tomorrow," he said. Apparently he got the hint and let the conversation die. "I'll walk you back to your room. You really do need to rest."

He was right, of course. She did need to rest to have the strength for what was to come. At her door she asked, "Where will you be sleeping?"

"I'll be down the hall," he said. "The other team members are right next door. You'll meet Drew and Samantha in the morning."

She put her hand on the doorknob but paused to ask, "Why are you doing this? I mean I know it's your job, but…"

"I want Santini. He killed my friend and has evaded authorities for too long. I won't rest until he's behind bars for the rest of his life."

She absorbed his words, understanding what drove him and appreciating that he'd shared his story with her. "I meant, letting me stay here? This seems above the call of duty."

One corner of his mouth curved up with the barest hint of a smile before he tamed his lips back into a straight line. "I promised you I'd keep you safe. This is as safe as it gets."

"Are you always so in control and contained?"

"That's the rumor." This time he did smile, revealing a dimple in his cheek.

Her breath stalled. He really was handsome, even more so when he smiled. That dimple was charming. She wondered what it would be like to have his charm turned fully on her. She placed a hand over her tummy to still the flutter of attraction that wanted to take flight. "Good night, Blake."

"Good night, Liz."

He walked away, disappearing into a room at the end of the hallway, leaving Liz alone with only her prayers for company.

No, that wasn't exactly true. Blake would be right down the hall if she needed him.

She'd never had anyone be there for her. She was the one to take care of others, seeing to everyone else's needs before her own. It was a part of her makeup, her genetic code, or at least that was what she'd been taught in her psychology classes in college. Those personality tests pegged her as a helper and a thinker, which stood to reason why it was so hard for her to let others help her. And why she overanalyzed everything.

Seeing to her safety was Blake's job, she reasoned. He needed her to capture Santini. And she needed Blake to rescue her sister. They were helping each other.

A win, win.

But why did she have the sinking feeling that what they both wanted would come with a price?

THREE

Liz awoke to a gray, stormy sky outside her window. Despite the ominous clouds overhead, the view from her room was as spectacular as she'd suspected.

The famed Horseshoe Falls were frozen, creating a wall of white. Though Liz knew from what she'd read about the falls when Jillian had first announced she and Travis would be eloping to Niagara and spending their honeymoon in the romantic setting, the water beneath the top layers of ice still flowed due to a steel boom ice catcher.

She wished she had a steel boom to catch Santini. The thought galvanized her to get ready for what lay ahead. Though fear threatened to sap her resolve, she had to forge forward. Her sister was counting on her. He dad was counting on her. She couldn't fail her father. She'd promised him she'd look out for Jillian. And she'd tried.

She clenched her jaw. If only Jillian had listened to her and not run off to marry Travis. But Jillian had always had a mind of her own and rarely listened to reason.

In fact she'd scoffed at Liz's attempts to keep her from making mistakes.

If I don't make mistakes then how will I learn if something is right for me or not?

Jillian's word echoed through Liz's mind. Well, hopefully, Jillian learned that Travis was a mistake, but what a painful way to learn that lesson. A lesson that had lifelong consequences. Marriage wasn't something to enter into lightly. And despite how easy it was to obtain a divorce, both Liz and Jillian had been taught that marriage was sacred, something to be honored and cherished. What was God's purpose for Jillian to marry a thief and a smuggler? A man obviously not of God.

Judge not, least ye be judged. The line of scripture ran through her head like tickertape, reminding her that it wasn't right for her to evaluate Travis's worth.

Still, the man had knowingly committed more than one crime.

Shaking her head with exasperation, Liz

selected a long tunic sweater in green over fleece-lined stretch pants tucked inside her winter boots. She was braiding her hair when she heard voices outside her room door.

Blake's deep tone she recognized. Two others, one male and the other female, she didn't recognize, but figured they were Drew and Samantha, whom Blake had mentioned last night.

After securing her long braid with a rubber band, she opened the door and entered the living room. Blake had his back to her, blocking her view of the two people with him. But then he turned around and captured her whole focus.

He'd changed into green cargo pants and a cream-colored cable knit sweater. He'd also taken the time to shave, which accentuated the planes and angles of his face. His dark hair was still damp. Liz liked the way the ends curled at his nape. Weariness rimmed his dark eyes. He gave her a quick once-over.

She caught something akin to interest in his expression, which seemed to thaw the hard coldness of his eyes just a tad more. Her heart bumped against her breastbone as attraction zinged through her veins and made her knees weak. Her mouth went dry. Confusion swirled within her brain. She never went all mushy over a man. Only heartache lay in that direction.

Watching her sister fall in love over and over again with various men through the years and then witnessing the emotional upheaval when the relationship ended had drilled home to Liz what she'd learned from watching her father after her mother's death. Love equaled pain.

Whether it was a bruised ego, as was often the case with Jillian, or a broken spirit like their father, giving one's heart away meant losing a part of oneself.

Liz had no intention of losing herself for anyone.

"Good morning." A hint of a smile touched his lips drawing her attention. He had such a nice-shaped mouth. She batted down that errant thought. "I hope you slept well."

She was surprised to realize she had. Knowing he was close had given her a sense of security. Physical security, that is. Certainly not emotional. If anything, he made her emotions more raw and tender. But he had protected her from danger, and she had no doubt he would again, if needed. That was his job. And he seemed to take his job ultraseriously.

"Yes, thank you." She straightened her spine and leaned to the side to see around him. A tall, good-looking man and a pretty, blond-haired woman smiled at her. "Hello."

Blake stepped aside. "This is Royal Canadian Mounted Police Inspector Drew Kelly and FBI liaison Samantha Kelly."

She noted the wedding rings on their fingers. A married couple. That was unexpected. And yet comforting. Though she wasn't sure why she felt comforted by the knowledge that these two were together. Maybe it had something to do with how pretty the petite woman was?

Whoa, what did that matter? Liz wasn't in competition for Blake's attention. She wasn't interested in him in that way.

The woman thrust out her hand. "Nice to meet you, Miss Cantrell. You can call me Sami."

Sami's bright blue eyes sparkled with curiosity. She wore gray wool pants and a charcoal-colored sweater that set off her creamy complexion. Her golden-blond hair was clipped back at her nape. She was a beautiful woman and made Liz feel dowdy in comparison. Self-consciously, Liz pushed the end of her braid off her shoulder so that it swung out of sight behind her.

Liz shook the woman's hand, liking her directness. "Likewise. And call me Liz, please."

"Miss Cantrell." Drew extended his hand, as well. He was a big man with wide shoulders beneath a flannel shirt. His brown hair was shorn in a close crop and his hazel eyes regarded her with kindness and a tinge of sympathy.

Liz shook the Canadian's massive hand, then retracted her own and tucked both hands behind her back. She sent Blake a curious look.

"The Kellys will help with the sting operation," Blake offered, apparently reading her unspoken question.

"The more hands on deck the better, right?" She was glad to know he wasn't above asking for help. Maybe he wasn't as much of a control freak as she'd first assumed.

"We'll be wiring you here rather than at the drop point." Sami picked up a black bag from where it sat on the coffee table.

Liz swallowed back a lump of trepidation. She was going to wear a wire? Like in the movies? Were they expecting her to actually talk to Santini?

She'd assumed she'd hand the necklace over and in exchange be given her sister without much fanfare. At least none until Blake and his team swooped in and arrested Santini for kidnapping and whatever other charges Blake had in store for the man. Liz's gaze jumped to Blake. "Why am I wearing a wire?"

"The more evidence we have against Santini the better." His impenetrable gaze dared her to challenge him. "Plus, it will give us a way to communicate with you."

His words made sense. She appreciated "just in case" thinking. "Okay, good."

Mild surprise flared in his eyes. Clearly he'd expected her to balk. She had to admit she got a little thrill from keeping him guessing. Which was so unlike her. She didn't play games or flirt. But for some reason she wanted to shake Blake out of his stoicism. She needed to nip that in the bud right now. He was not her concern. They would be parting ways as soon as they found her sister.

Focus on Jillian! she silently scolded herself.

"Great," Blake said. "Drew and I will get breakfast started while you ladies..." He waved a hand toward the bedroom Liz had vacated, clearly unsure what to say.

Sami laughed. "Wow, I've never seen you flustered, Blake. It's refreshing."

He gave her a scowl then strode toward the kitchen.

Sami grinned and motioned for Liz to follow her back into the bedroom.

Liz was grateful to have a female attending her, which was far better than letting Blake help her. She wouldn't give in to the pull she felt for the handsome agent. She needed to keep her focus on Jillian and the danger ahead. Letting herself be distracted put Jillian, herself and everyone else in greater jeopardy.

Sami unzipped the bag and took out a thin wire with a pea-sized ball at the end. "We'll tape this to your chest. It will record any conversation and allow us to hear what's going on. You'll be given an ear piece so you can hear Blake's instructions." She smiled. "And don't worry, the tape comes off easily without taking any skin."

"Good to know." The whole situation seemed so surreal. Here she was being wired by an FBI agent in an attempt to trap a crime boss and rescue her sister from his evil clutches. It was almost as if she'd stepped into an action flick or one of her favorite author's crime novels. "How long have you been with the FBI?"

"I was accepted into the academy right after college," Sami replied. "I'd majored in criminal justice so I made a good candidate for the bureau."

"Blake had said you're a liaison?"

"Actually an assistant to the legal attaché, but since Drew was coming to help Blake, I convinced my boss to let me offer support since this involves both of our countries plus Venezuela."

"How long have you two been married?"

A tender smile touched Sami's lips. "Almost six months."

A strange ache in the vicinity of her heart made Liz look away. She didn't understand what she was feeling. Envy? But she'd never experienced envy when her college friends married one after the other until she was the last one still single. It didn't make sense now. She chalked up the odd sensation to nerves and fear. The situation she found herself in would wreak havoc on anyone's emotions.

"How did you meet?" Liz asked to keep her mind off what she was feeling inside.

Sami's hands stilled for a moment. "I was hunting a serial killer who murdered my childhood best friend. I was determined to solve her murder and discovered that her killer had killed before on both sides of the northern border. When the man I was tracking crossed into Drew's jurisdiction, our agencies allowed us to form a joint investigation. I dubbed the killer 'Birdman' because of the bird symbol on the clue he left at each crime scene."

Liz gaped at the woman, not even sure what to say. Sympathy for Sami's loss crowded Liz's chest. She couldn't imagine what that sort of job would entail and wasn't she sure wanted to know any more details. "Did you catch him?"

A look of triumph crossed Sami's face. "We did, but it wasn't easy."

Liz stifled a shiver. "It must be hard with you both having such demanding and…risky careers."

Sami cocked her head. "Some days, but I wouldn't trade even one day of my life with Drew for a million without him. I took the job with the legal attaché so that I could live in Vancouver, British Columbia, with Drew. After our wedding, we bought a house where someday we'll raise our kids. We're careful when we're out in the field and are grateful for every day we have together because we know how easily and quickly life can spin out of control. God willing, we'll grow old and reminisce about our adventures to our grandchildren and great-grandchildren." She scrunched up her nose. "We'll leave the details out."

Again, that bizarre twinge made Liz's chest hurt beneath the spot where Sami patted down the tape over the little microphone. "Jillian wanted to start a family, but now…" She pressed her lips together for a second as a wave of anger washed over her. "Travis wasn't such a great catch."

"I'm sorry your sister was taken by Santini." Sami stepped back to let Liz dress. "But we'll get her back."

"I'm counting on it," Liz replied. "Blake convinced me to trust him." She let out a rough scoff. "Or rather threatened me with jail if I didn't."

"He's all talk."

"I don't know." She remembered the intense way he'd stared her down in the interrogation room. "He seemed pretty serious about it."

"That's just his way. Though I'll admit he

can be intimidating," Sami agreed. "However, once he relaxes a bit, he's not so bad."

"He relaxes?" Liz couldn't imagine it. The man appeared so buttoned down and rigid. But that brief smile earlier lingered in her mind. She'd like to see him fully smile again. To hear him laugh. Would he have a deep laugh? She couldn't imagine him laughing. "That I'd like to see."

Her breath caught on the admission. No, she wouldn't, she silently scolded herself. She wanted this situation over and done with so she never had to see Blake or the inside of an interrogation room again.

She wanted to go back to her quiet life on Hilton Head Island, back to the store and her own home with her sister where the only excitement she had to contend with were the tourists who came during the warmer seasons or the storms that blew through off the Atlantic.

Liz and Sami left the bedroom and joined the same Canada Border Services officer Liz had met last night at the dining table. Nathanial Longhorn stood and hurried around the table to pull out Liz's chair. "Miss Cantrell, you're looking lovely."

"Thank you," she murmured, appreciating

his manners and his compliment though she knew he was only being polite.

He sat across from her, leaving the chair next to her open for Blake who carried over a platter stacked with pancakes.

"Here ya'll go. Dig in," Blake said, setting the platter of steaming warm cakes on the table next to the carafe of coffee and a pitcher of orange juice.

Drew brought over a plate piled with link sausages, offering them to his wife first. Sami's adoring smile brought a lump to Liz's throat.

Blake sat down beside her, bumping her knee as he did. "Sorry."

"No problem." She adjusted her legs away from him and rubbed at the spot on her knee that felt branded by the accidental touch.

As they ate they discussed the details of the plan. By the time their appetites were sated, Liz had the particulars of her part of the plan memorized though she'd had to argue a few points. She'd enter the fort alone—Blake had wanted to accompany her but she'd argued Santini probably knew who Blake was and would recognize him. Blake conceded the point.

Then she would head for the middle of the

fort yard and wait for Santini's next contact. Blake and his team would be on scene hidden from sight but covering the entrance and exit, all the while keeping a close eye on her.

On the ride to the fort, she was struck by Blake's easy command of his vehicle as he diced his way through the morning traffic. He was probably in easy command of most things in his life. She wondered what had compelled him to become an ICE agent, and then doggedly chased the wondering away.

She didn't need to know about Blake Fallon. Didn't want to know. She needed to keep her concentration on the task at hand. Saving her sister.

She didn't want to become some starry-eyed ninny following after her "man."

Yet the image of happily married Sami and Drew floated through her mind. There was no way anyone could accuse Sami of being starry-eyed or a ninny. The woman was an FBI agent and had successfully stopped a serial killer. She was strong and competent, a woman Liz could admire. Yet, Liz worried what would happen to Sami if something horrible happened to Drew. Or vice versa. The risk of heartache was enough to make Liz's throat ache.

She was grateful for some distance when Blake dropped her off at a bus stop a mile from the entrance to the fort. She noted the worry in his eyes, and for some reason his concern made her feel cared for. Dumb for her to think that. He was only worried she'd blow the sting operation somehow, and that Santini would slip through his hands again. Right?

She boarded the next bus per their plan and got off in front of the long path leading to Fort George. She quickly made the trek and entered the fort, which was walled by a wooden fence. Inside the enclosure, large expanses of lawn dusted white with snow spread out between buildings that retained their 1800s charm. She paid to enter and roamed the center of the fort, wondering when and where Santini would show up.

She glanced at her watch. It was close to noon. Close to the time she was to ransom her sister's life for the diamond necklace tucked in her mother's beautiful box and then inside a shopping bag clutched in her hand.

The wire taped to her chest itched. Liz poked at the device in irritation.

"Stop fidgeting," Blake admonished in her ear through the communication link.

It was weird having him in her head and his gaze on her as well, though she had no idea where he'd positioned himself. She smoothed back her hair, wondering what he saw when he looked at her. Did he see how scared she was? How uncertain? Could he see the blush creeping up her neck at knowing he was watching her every move? This off-kilter feeling made her edgy. She shouldn't care what he thought of her. This was about Jillian.

She dropped her hand to her side and scanned the crowd milling about the historic Fort George. The fort employees were dressed in period costumes and several were leading small groups on tours.

She'd read the brochure last night before finally falling into a dreamless sleep. As a history buff, she'd found the rich history of the fort and the surrounding area fascinating. She lifted the brochure she'd brought with her to her mouth to hide the fact she was speaking. "Did you know during the War of 1812, this fort served as the headquarters for the Centre Division of the British army?"

"No, I didn't," Blake responded. "I must have missed that in history class."

Her lips twisted. She moved to a plaque pretending to read it. "Well, considering this is a part of Canada's history and since you're from the South, you wouldn't have been given this tidbit of information."

"What makes you think I'm from the South?"

"I've an ear for accents. Plus, you dropped a ya'll this morning. It was kind of hard to miss."

He actually chuckled in her ear.

She was so surprised her hand loosened around the bag and she almost dropped it. "Did you just laugh?"

"Maybe."

She pressed her lips together to keep from smiling and slipped the brochure into the bag.

Someone brushed against her. Startled, she jumped back a step. Remembering the last time someone had bumped into her, she swung around, ready to jab her assailant in the nose.

A short, older woman wearing a heavy coat and a hat pulled down low over her ears, allowing little tufts of dark hair to poke out, blinked at her.

"My apologies." The woman reached out a hand to steady Liz and pressed a piece of paper in Liz's hand before hurrying away. A note!

Liz unfolded the paper. "That woman passed me a note that says to be at Butler's Barracks in five minutes." Her heart revved up. Would she find Jillian there? She dug out the fort's brochure and consulted the map to see where the barracks were located.

"Sit tight, Liz," Blake instructed. "Drew will detain that woman and see what she knows."

"It says be there in five minutes." She found the barracks on the map and rushed in its direction. "I'm heading there now."

"I need to get people in place over there," he said, his voice sharp.

"And I told you I'd do whatever is necessary to get my sister back," she replied just as sharply. "So you'd better hurry."

She heard his frustrated growl but didn't let it deter her. When she reached the barracks she skidded to a halt, scanning the few people wandering around. An older couple walked with arms linked, heads bent together. A group of school children and their chaperones gathered near a cannon on display while they listened to a fort employee no doubt explaining the use of cannon fire in the 1800s.

No one seemed the least bit interested in her.

A piece of paper flapping against the barracks door caught her attention. She moved swiftly to the door and read the note pinned there out loud.

"Leave the necklace. Your sister will be at the hotel."

"Okay, I've got eyes on you," Blake said. "Place the bag on the doorstep and head back to the entrance."

"You'll take me back to the hotel?" she asked, still clutching the bag.

He sighed. "I'll send Nathanial."

Something in his tone stirred a riot of apprehension in her chest. Careful to conceal her mouth with one hand, she said, "You don't believe she'll be there, do you?"

"Honestly, no," Blake answered. "Our best course of action is to follow whoever retrieves the bag and pray they lead us to Santini. And your sister."

In other words, he didn't believe Santini would honor his word or show up. The man was a ruthless criminal, so that opinion wasn't surprising. That thought led to another. Did Blake also think that it was too late for Jillian?

A sharp, knifelike pain slid through Liz's midsection. She loathed being at anyone's mercy. And right now she was at everyone's mercy. Santini, who threatened to kill her sister and may have already done so. And Blake, who, while she appreciated his honesty, was still calling the shots.

The stress of not knowing if her sister lived or had died gnawed away at her, making the breakfast she'd eaten turn in her stomach. Desperate, she did the only thing she could—trusted Blake to do his job.

From his perch on a corner bastion of the fort's palisade, Blake watched Liz closely as she struggled to come to terms with his pronouncement. Her shoulders drooped and the distress so clearly etched on her pretty face made his insides clench.

He wanted to go to her to ease the pain she was suffering.

The need caught him by surprise.

He wasn't one for demonstrative feelings. Just like his father. Doug Fallon was a hard man, an even harder cop who'd admonished his son that only weaklings let their feelings show. Which was why Blake's mom had bailed on him and his dad, taking Blake's little sister with her. She'd wanted to feel loved. She hadn't.

Even knowing he needed to keep his emotions in check, he couldn't help the protective urges coursing through his system. After their conversation last night, he'd realized how much Liz had given, had sacrificed, for her family. Respect and admiration filled him.

She'd been so young to become caregiver and surrogate parent to her younger sister. That couldn't have been easy. Teens in general were riddled with angst, but one who'd lost both parents must have been a handful. Well, from all accounts, Jillian was a handful. But she was Liz's only family. It stood to reason why Liz was so determined to protect her.

He hoped with everything in him that he could deliver on his promise to rescue Jillian.

For Liz's sake.

For his own sake.

Failure wasn't an option.

He'd failed to provide backup to his fellow ICE agent Liam at a critical moment that had cost the agent his life at the hands of Santini.

Blake couldn't let the attraction that sizzled between him and Liz complicate the situation.

Though he had to admit to himself he found her unassuming beauty very alluring. She seemed to not even notice the effect she had on men. He'd watched every male on the fort grounds turn to watch her as she walked

FOUR

Liz struggled against the hands dragging her into the barracks. The bag holding the necklace flew from her grip to land several feet away. Panic beat a desperate drum inside her chest and she let out a howl, and then another, but the wooden walls absorbed her screams. She jabbed and kicked at her assailant.

In her ear she could hear Blake's assurances he was coming to rescue her. But would he arrive in time? Would her attacker kill her and make off with the jewels before Blake could reach her?

Breath-stealing panic rose like a choking tide. She didn't want to die. What would happen to Jillian? Who would fight for her life if Liz were dead?

A line of scripture flashed through her mind—"I can do all things through Christ who strengthens me."

Please, Lord, give me strength.

With renewed determination, she used the heel of her boot to stomp hard on her captor's instep.

A deep male voice swore and shoved her toward the back wall. She stumbled, catching herself on the edge of a wooden-frame cot. Light from the many windows revealed a long room with a row of similar cots lining one wall and a bench table where a man dressed in period garb was seated hunched over a plate of food. Not a man, but a mannequin, she realized. The barracks were festooned to look like they would have in the 1800s. A fireplace that had once burned with flame was dark and cold. Leaning against the side of the fireplace was a black fire iron. She raced to pick it up to use as a weapon and whirled around to face her attacker.

Recognition made her jaw drop. "Travis?"

He looked disheveled in wrinkled corduroy pants and a dress shirt beneath a wool coat. Several days growth of stubble shadowed his jaw. His bloodshot gaze watched her warily. "It's me. I'm sorry I scared you. Put that down."

"No way." She hadn't trusted him before this debacle; she certainly didn't trust him now. Her attention zeroed in on the bag containing her mother's box and the necklace where it had landed in the far corner behind Travis before her gaze skittered back to her brother-in-law. "Where's Jillian? Is she at the hotel like Santini promised?"

Travis shook his head. "No, I don't think so. I don't know where she is. He separated us." His voice quivered. "I was told to come here, retrieve the necklace and then he'd contact me."

"Figures." Blake was right that Santini would lie. She was so naive to think a criminal would keep his word.

"But I wanted you to know I'm doing everything I can to rescue her," Travis assured her. "You have to trust me."

Again, another man telling her she had to trust him without giving her any reason to. Unbelievable.

The door to the barracks burst open, and Blake barreled inside with his gun drawn, his gaze sweeping over them. He slammed the door closed behind him. Liz didn't hesitate to take advantage of the distraction. She leaped over the next cot and grabbed the bag with the diamond necklace from the floor.

Though Blake kept his gun trained on

Travis, he darted an anxious look toward her. "Are you okay?"

"Yes." She clutched the bag to her chest. "This is Travis, my no-good, rotten brother-in-law."

Travis's wide eyes swung from Blake to her. "You called the police?" He groaned, a lamenting sound that pummeled Liz. "If Santini finds out—" Travis bent forward, putting his hands on his knees. His breathing turned ragged "—she's as good as dead."

Liz gritted her teeth against the slicing pain of his words. She'd placed her trust in Blake and his team. She needed to hold on to the hope that there was still a chance of rescuing Jillian before it was too late.

Blake stalked forward. "Where's Santini?"

Travis jerked upright and backed up. "I don't know. He took Jillian and told me to come here for the necklace."

"And then what are you supposed to do?" Blake pressed.

Travis hesitated.

Obviously, he didn't want to help the police. Anger swept through Liz, heating her chilled skin. Her fingers tightened around the bag. "If you love Jillian then you'll help us."

Travis's gaze darted between her and

Blake. Indecision warred in his eyes. Finally, he nodded. "I want immunity."

Blake scoffed. "It doesn't work like that. I don't have the authority to agree to immunity. But I will say your helping us will go a long way to making a better deal for yourself. Less prison time."

Travis licked his lips as he contemplated Blake's words. Liz held her breath, praying he'd make the right choice. The only choice that would help her sister.

Finally Travis said, "I'm to wait at a diner in town. He'll contact me there with further instructions."

Liz breathed out a small measure of relief. Okay, they were one step closer to finding her sister. Still, she wasn't about to let Travis off the hook. "How could you let this happen? You're supposed to protect her!"

Travis swiped a hand through his brown hair. "It wasn't supposed to go down like this. I do love Jillian. I only wanted to give her something tangible, something I thought she'd find interesting. I didn't think Santini would miss the necklace. There were so many others, better ones, in the shipment. I thought it was just rocks strung together with some gold wire until he showed up in our hotel room. How was I supposed to know it was uncut diamonds? I'd never seen them before. If I'd known I never would have taken it. Especially if I'd thought for a second that Santini would come after Jillian for it. You have to believe me, I never meant to hurt Jillian."

"Hurt? He hurt her?" she squeaked the words out. *Oh, no. Please, Lord, no.*

Travis grimaced. "You know Jillian. She doesn't take well to being told what to do."

Oh, Jillian. Liz did know. Her little sister had spent too many years getting her way as both Liz and their father tried to make up for the loss of their mother. It made Jillian unbearable at times. Tears pricked the backs of Liz's eyes. "Please tell me she's alive."

"Yes, she is, but if I don't bring that necklace back to Santini he'll kill her." Travis's face twisted. "And then me."

Of course he was concerned about his own skin. Bitterness clogged Liz's throat. "This is all your fault. If you weren't working for a criminal, if you weren't a thief, my sister would be safe at home with me."

"I know, I know." He spread his hands wide. "I want to make this right."

"The only way this will ever be right is

when Jillian is set free," she said. "But you and Santini both belong in jail."

Something hard flashed in Travis's brown eyes before his shoulders slumped. "You're right. I don't deserve Jillian. She's the best thing that has ever happened to me. I love her. I have to get her away from Santini." He stepped toward Liz, holding out his hand. "Please, give me the necklace."

She stepped back. "You take me to my sister."

"I would if I could," Travis said.

"Which mine did the necklace come from?" Blake asked, drawing their attention. He'd been quiet during her and Travis's exchange, possibly taking Travis's measure, or perhaps her own. What went on behind the implacable mask he wore?

Turning his focus to Blake, Travis shrugged. "Hey, I don't work the mines. I've never even seen one. All I do is transport the stuff I'm handed once I'm in the country."

He made it sound so easy and civil. She'd read and seen the news reports about blood diamonds in developing nations. It sickened her to know that so much immorality existed in the world. Liz's lip curled. "Do you have any idea of the working conditions of the men, women and children who work in the mines in Venezuela or Sierra Leone or the Congo? Don't you have a conscience?"

"It's not personal, it's business," Travis said in a tone that suggested she was the one in the wrong.

Disgusted by him, she turned to Blake. "So now what?"

"Now our plan has changed," Blake said. "He'll wear the wire and meet with Santini." He turned his dark-eyed gaze on Travis, who visibly blanched.

"No way, man," Travis said. "He finds a wire on me, I'm done for."

Blake's gaze narrowed. "He won't find it. All you have to do is get Santini to incriminate himself. Get him to admit to funding the mines in Venezuela, to smuggling the unregistered diamonds and to kidnapping Jillian. Then we'll move in and take him down." He turned to Liz. "And free your sister."

That sounded good to Liz. But her frayed nerves wouldn't be soothed until she was reunited with her sister. And then she and Jillian would leave this place of snow and ice and head back to the peace and quiet of Hilton Head. At least when a storm blew in there she was prepared. This storm she'd found herself in right here right now was like nothing she'd experienced before and there'd been no way to prepare.

But the crisis wasn't over yet. And she had no idea what to expect next. Or whether or not Jillian would live or die.

"I'll call for a taxi to take you back to the safe house," Blake said, anxious to get moving. They were close to bringing down Santini and rescuing Liz's sister. He could feel it in his bones. But he had to get Liz somewhere safe. Her presence was too distracting for him. When she was close, she was all he could concentrate on. Not good at all.

They were standing in a secluded spot in an alley behind a strip mall where there were no prying eyes. Drew and Sami waited in an SUV nearby with Travis in the backseat. They'd transferred the wire from Liz to Travis with little fuss. The plan was to drop Travis off a few blocks from the café and then stake out the diner.

When Santini showed, they'd swoop in. Or if Travis was instructed to go to another rendezvous spot, they would follow. There would come a moment when Santini would come out from under whatever rock he'd crawled beneath, and Blake would be ready.

"No way, I'm coming with you. My sister's trusting me to help." Liz stared down her nose at Blake. He almost laughed at her attempt to intimidate him. Her honey-colored braid was coming loose, and her cheeks were pink from the cold. She stomped her feet to keep warm. "And if you try to leave me behind, I'll just follow you."

Blake clenched his back teeth. He wanted her to cooperate and go back to the condo and let his team do what they did best. But from the stubborn jut of her chin and the determination in the depths of her sea-colored gaze he knew that wasn't going to happen.

He understood and even appreciated her commitment to rescuing her sister. But she was a distraction he didn't need. After fearing he'd failed her back at Fort George, then the surge of relief and…something else that he refused to acknowledge when he'd entered the barracks to find her holding off her brother-in-law with an iron poker, he knew having her around wasn't in anyone's best interest. Certainly not his.

He didn't do emotions. He wouldn't let any

weakness stop him from doing his job. Especially on a mission. Getting tangled up inside over a woman could lead to disaster. If he started putting her welfare ahead of the mission's goal, then failure was guaranteed. And that he couldn't abide.

But the guilt riding on his back told him he should never have let her get that close to danger. He should put her on the next plane back to her island home where she would be safe and out of his hair. For both their sakes.

Yet, he admitted to himself, he'd do just about anything to bring down Santini, including saddling himself with this headstrong, attractive, maddening woman. He owed Liam that. The sting of remorse was never far from the surface, reminding Blake of the debt he must pay.

"Fine," he ground out. "But no matter what, you aren't leaving the car."

"Okay, I won't get in the way." She turned on her heel to march to his sedan and slid into the passenger seat.

Shaking his head and holding on to his patience, Blake climbed behind the steering wheel. With the heater on full blast, he followed the Kellys' SUV, stopping a few cars

back as they let Travis out. Blake kept an eye
on the man in case he tried to run with the
necklace as they slowly trailed him.

Liz had handed over the paper bag easily
enough, much to Blake's surprise. He had
figured she'd want to keep control of the
necklace. He hoped it was a sign that she
trusted him. Trust meant she'd act when he
told her to, which could be the difference between life and death. That she'd understood
that he was the professional and allowed him
to do what he needed to in order to get the
job done.

He found a parking spot with an unob-
structed view of the diner's front door as
Travis entered the eatery carrying the bag.
Nathanial was already inside and would
have eyes on Travis. Blake turned up the vol-
ume on the receiver that permitted them to
hear when Santini contacted Travis. Normal
sounds of silverware clanking on dishes and
the hum of conversations filled the interior
of the sedan.

Drumming his fingers on the steering
wheel, Blake ignored the floral scent of Liz's
shampoo that scented the enclosed space.
He'd noticed it this morning as well, but now
it was softer, more alluring.

The sound of a cell phone ringing made Blake's shoulders tense. "Here we go," he murmured.

Travis's voice came over the receiver. "Yes. I have it. Where's Jillian? No, I want to talk to Jillian. Where is she? Fine. I'll bring the necklace." Travis repeated the address aloud. "Please don't hurt Jillian." The pleading tone in Travis's voice sounded genuine before he ended the call. Then he groaned. "Did you hear that?" His question was obviously aimed at Blake and Liz. "They're holding her at some warehouse."

Blake dialed Travis's number and got him on the line. "Stay put. We'll come to you."

"Santini said within the hour," Travis complained. "I need to take the necklace to him. Now."

"Understood," Blake said. He needed to buy some time for Nathanial to coordinate with local law enforcement to take Travis into custody.

Blake opened his tablet and quickly typed in the street name on a map of Niagara and found the building, a sixteen-thousand-square-foot structure off Highway 420 near the Niagara Centre for the Arts. Liz leaned over to see the screen, bringing with her another wave of her captivating scent to tease his nose and fire his senses.

"Is that far?" she asked.

He realized he was staring at her well-formed mouth, on the little freckle near the corner of her upper lip. Whoa. Not okay. He forced his attention away from her pretty face and back to the tablet screen. "Not far. A few miles."

She nodded and straightened, giving him much-needed space to clear his head. A total distraction. One he didn't need. He couldn't let her affect him. It could be dangerous for all of them. Bolstering his resolve, he squared his shoulders and got back to business.

He called Drew and relayed the information. "Nathanial will coordinate with the local law and take Travis into custody." He slanted a glance at Liz. "I'm also going to have an officer escort Liz back to the condo."

"No!" She protested. "I need to go with you."

He shook his head but spoke to Drew. "I'll be right behind you." He hung up and then shifted to face an irate Liz. "Look, this could get very hairy and I don't want to have to worry about you when I need to be focused on rescuing your sister."

"I'll stay in the car," she said.

A commotion over the receiver drew their attention.

"Hey, stop!" That was Nathanial. "Travis!"

They could hear a scuffle, a grunt and then nothing.

Blake's phone buzzed. Nathanial. He answered. "What's happening?"

Nathanial's voice sounded winded. "He ran through the kitchen and out the back door, but I snagged him before he could get away."

Irritation exploded in Blake's chest. If Travis had escaped, he'd have taken off with the only leverage they had, the necklace. "On my way," he said and started the sedan's engine.

Liz jammed her hands into her coat pocket. "I knew he'd try something like that."

Sparing her a quick glance, he noted the anger sparking in her eyes. It matched the fire in his own gut. He drove to the back alley where Nathanial had Travis on the ground and had zip-tied his hands together. A Niagara Regional Police cruiser shot down the alley from the other direction and pulled to a stop at the same time as Blake. Another cruiser followed suit behind the first one.

Liz hopped out before Blake could turn off the engine. Her impulsiveness could be her downfall. She ran to grab the bag from where it rested near Travis's prone body.

Blake jumped out of the car and stalked over to Travis and hauled him to his feet. "Really? Where did you think you were going to go?"

Blake handed Travis off to a uniformed Niagara officer. "Take him in. I'll have my boss call your chief to discuss what to do with him."

The officer dragged Travis toward the cruiser.

"Wait! You gotta let me help!" he screamed. "Santini will see you coming and kill Jillian. Let me—" The officer forced him into the back of the car and slammed the door shut, cutting off Travis's pleas.

Liz hugged the bag to her chest. "We're wasting time. We need to go."

"We are going," Blake said pointing to himself and Nathanial.

"Blake," Liz implored. "I need to be there."

He shook his head. No, she didn't. He didn't want her there. He wanted to be able to have all his focus on the job and not on her safety. Not when he felt so connected to every nuance of her mood, her thoughts. Crazy. They hardly knew each other yet there was something between them that set him off balance.

Nathanial held out his hand. "I'll take the necklace."

She hesitated before releasing her hold on the bag and letting Nathanial take possession of the evidence they would use to help put Santini behind bars once and for all.

Aware they did indeed need to get a move on, Blake waved over another uniformed officer. "You, on the other hand, are going with…" Blake glanced at the man's badge and read his name. "Officer Abelin, please escort Miss Cantrell to this address." He stated the street and number as the officer wrote it down. "And if for any reason she gives you any trouble, take her to your precinct and hold her."

"Please, don't do this." Her eyes implored him to relent but he couldn't for her sake as well as his own. "Please. I promise I won't get in the way."

"I know you won't, you'll be at the condo where I know you'll be safe," he replied. Hating to see the distress in her eyes, he softened his tone and took her hands in his. "I promise I'll bring Jillian straight to you. You'll have to trust me."

Her jaw set into a hard line and she tugged her hands free. "Right. Because what other choice do I have?"

He wasn't sure how to make this easier for her. And wasting time trying to figure it out served no purpose. "Officer."

Officer Abelin nodded and cupped her elbow. "This way, miss."

Blake watched as Liz was led past Travis in the back of the cruiser.

One hurdle taken care of. Now to find Santini's lair and rescue Jillian Cantrell. Blake was determined to make good on his promise to Liz that he'd bring her sister back to her unharmed.

He didn't even want to think about what he would do if he had to tell Liz he'd failed.

Liz slid into the backseat of the police car, seething with frustration as Blake and Nathanial drove away, leaving her behind. She fisted her hands on her thighs. She hated this feeling of helplessness. This feeling of being dismissed. It shouldn't upset her. Blake was doing his job. She was a civilian, not equipped to help. That was little comfort. She had no control of the situation. She couldn't influence the outcome.

But that wasn't true. She could pray.

At the moment that was all the power she had. All the power she needed. Faith had to be enough. Because without faith, there was no hope. And without hope, what was the point?

She bowed her head and asked God for protection for Jillian. For Blake and his team. She prayed Santini would be taken into custody and they'd never have to fear him again.

Shouting broke through her reverie. She glanced up in time to see Travis slam the butt of a gun into Officer Abelin's skull. The officer went down in a heap. Travis grabbed the car door handle and yanked the door open.

"Get out," he shouted, waving the gun.

"How did you…?" She was sure his hands had been secured behind his back with zip ties.

"Come on," he yelled.

She scrambled out of the car and saw the other officer lying unconscious on the ground. Fear mushroomed inside of her. "Is he dead?"

Travis gripped her by the elbow. "Naw, just out cold. I may be a thief but I'm not a killer. Yet." He tossed the gun into the backseat and then pulled her down the alley. "We're going to call that cop and tell him to bring me that necklace or both of the Cantrell sisters' lives will be on his head."

FIVE

The warehouse was empty. Frustration intensified the headache pounding Blake's brain. He stood in the wide-open expanse of what had once been a machine shop and raked his gaze over the grease-stained concrete floors and corrugated walls. There was no evidence that Santini and his gang of thugs had ever been here. Had Travis sent them on a wild-goose chase? Or had Santini planned to ambush Travis?

"Any activity at the perimeter?" he asked into the microphone attached to his flak vest.

"None." Drew's voice sounded in Blake's ear. "It's all quiet. What about inside?"

"Nothing to indicate Santini was here." Irritation burned through his gut. "Let's wrap this up. I want a word with Travis." By now Travis should be in a holding cell at the Niagara Regional Police station. Travis was going to regret crossing them. Any chance for a deal no longer existed.

Blake stalked out of the warehouse. He didn't relish informing Liz they were no closer to finding Santini or rescuing her sister. Travis had betrayed their trust. Overhead, dark clouds loomed and the temperature had dropped by several degrees. The crisp air signaled that a storm was brewing. Perfect. As if this operation couldn't get any more dismal.

Nathanial jogged over. "Hey, we have a problem."

"Yes, we do," Blake said. "Travis lied. Santini's not here."

Nathanial's lips thinned. "Yeah, well, then you're going to hate this. He got away from the officer who was transporting him to the local police station."

"He escaped?" The news socked Blake in the gut. "Unbelievable. How? His hands were zipped behind his back."

"Apparently he was able to bring his hands forward under his legs and break the zips and then put the officer out with a choke hold," Nathanial said. "But it gets worse."

Blake braced himself. Travis hadn't seemed like the murdering type, but then again, he'd duped Blake into believing that he could be trusted. "Did he kill the officer?"

"No, thankfully."

A blessing. "Then, what?"

"Travis also took out the officer escorting Liz to the condo."

A boulder-sized lump of dread thumped Blake's chest. He'd left her with the officer, confident she was protected, but he'd been wrong. So wrong. If something happened to her because he'd failed to provide the proper safety measures he'd never forgive himself. "Is she okay?" *Please, God let her be okay.*

"As far as witnesses can tell, yes, she's un-hurt," Nathanial said. "Travis stole a car and took Liz with him."

Fear slammed through Blake, bruising his heart. "How long ago?

"Thirty minutes max."

Blake clenched his fists. If Travis harmed her… there wouldn't be a rock large enough for Travis to hide under. Blake grabbed his cell and called Liz's number. The phone rang twice before Travis answered. "Agent Fallon, good timing. We were just about to call you."

Blake put the call on speaker so Nathanial could listen. "What have you done with Liz?" Blake barked.

"She's here with me."

Blake ground his jaw so hard his teeth ached. "You better not hurt her," he ground out. The thought of Liz injured or worse, dead, stole his breath.

"Bring me the necklace and I won't have to," Travis said. "Understand this, Agent Fallon, I will do anything to free Jillian. Including giving Liz to Santini in exchange for my wife. But I'd rather give him the necklace so both of the Cantrell sisters can walk away from this unharmed."

A riot of panic put Blake in a choke hold. "Where are you?"

"Meet us at the ice cream shop on Victoria Avenue." Travis hung up.

Blake wanted to pound his fist into something. This shouldn't have happened. He'd promised to protect Liz. She was having a hard enough time trusting him, and now he'd let her down. How was he ever going to live with that?

"Why are you doing this?" Liz demanded of Travis as he dragged her away from the stolen car and down the street toward the ice cream parlor where they were to meet Blake. A chill slithered over the collar of her coat and snaked down her spine. She shivered uncontrollably.

"You're only making things worse for yourself and not helping Jillian." Her voice came out wobbly from both the cold and the fear that trembled inside of her.

"I'm doing this for Jillian," Travis insisted. "You don't know Santini. There's no way he'll let her live if he doesn't get that necklace."

"How do you know Blake hasn't already arrested Santini?"

Sweat beaded on his upper lip. He wiped it away with the back of his hand. "Because I sent them to a bogus address."

"What?" She dug in her heels, forcing Travis to pause. She didn't understand this man. He just kept making one bad decision after another. Blake would be furious when he realized Travis had deceived him. "Why would you do that? Are you crazy?"

Travis's fingers dug into her biceps and pushed her to keep moving. "Santini would spot the cops long before they could get anywhere near him, and he'd kill Jillian without a second thought. I couldn't let that happen."

His dire pronouncement made Liz's heart spasm. "Where did Santini tell you to go?"

"Not to that warehouse," Travis replied.

Frustrated, she said, "Is he waiting now? You're playing with Jillian's life."

"This isn't a game," Travis snapped.

"No it's not. The only real chance we have of getting my sister back safely is for you to work with Blake," Liz implored. "Give him the right information so they can rescue Jillian."

"No, it's my job to rescue her," Travis said. "I'm her husband."

"Who put her in her danger to begin with," Liz pointed out. "You need to think this through, Travis. Your way hasn't worked. You need to let Blake and his team do their job. They are trained for this sort of thing. They know what they are doing."

At least she prayed and hoped they did. Blake had told her to trust him. And deep inside her trust of the ICE agent was growing, not just because the alternative was too hard to think about, but because of the kind of man he was beginning to prove himself to be. She wasn't equipped to negotiate the release of her sister. And though she was naive to the criminal world, she was smart enough to know once Santini had the diamond necklace in his hands, he'd have no reason to honor his word and let Jillian go. He might even kill her as a warning to others.

An anxious knot lodged itself in her midsection. "Please, Travis, cooperate with Blake."

The bell over the door chimed as they entered the parlor. The temperature inside wasn't much warmer than outside. Liz flexed her hands, wishing she had on gloves. Only one woman manned the ice cream cases. Considering it was colder outside than in the parlor, Liz wasn't surprised there were no customers. Not exactly ice cream weather.

"Be right with you," she said as she finished wiping the glass on the refrigerator behind her.

Travis shoved Liz into a chair by the window. He took the seat next to her and gazed outside with a pensive expression that made Liz hopeful he was reconsidering his plan. If he even had one. Leave it to Jillian to pick a man like Travis—a rootless slacker.

The doors opened with the melodic chime announcing a new patron. Liz swiveled, expecting to see Blake, but instead a tall man wearing a fedora and dark sunglasses entered. Which was odd since there was no sun out.

Disappointment that it wasn't Blake spread through her, followed quickly by apprehension. There was something familiar about the man in the fedora. Hadn't Blake said the man at the airport had on a fedora?

Beside her Travis stiffened and then swore.

The stranger sauntered over, his hands shoved into the pockets of his navy pea coat. He stopped beside the table and towered over them. "Where is it, Travis?"

Liz immediately recognized the voice. This was Santini's rival for the necklace. The same man who'd accosted her in her apartment and then later at the airport. Her tension ratcheted up several degrees. She shrank away until her back hit the window, the cold glass like ice. Liz's gaze met the woman's behind the counter, and Liz mouthed, *help me*. The woman's eyes widened, and fear crossed her face as she reached for the phone, hopefully to call for help.

Come on, Blake. Where are you?

"Ken, what are you doing here?" Travis rose to face the man.

"I want the necklace you bragged about."

"You don't want to get mixed up in this, Ken," Travis said, his voice low and intent. "Santini went ballistic when he learned I'd lifted the thing. Go back to Miami."

"I'm not worried about Santini," Ken said. "Santini is your problem."

Travis shook his head. "You should be worried. Santini is the problem of whoever has the necklace. If he finds out you're after it... let's just say he'll make sure you regret it like he has me."

Ken gestured to Liz. "She's working with the cops, dude."

"Yeah, I know." Travis swiped a hand through his hair. "Look, you really need to leave now."

"Not without the necklace."

Travis spread his hands wide. "It's not here."

Ken grabbed Travis by the collar of his jacket. "I didn't come all this way not to get my hands on those uncut diamonds. Where is it?"

Travis shrugged his hands up. "I told you, dude, it's not here."

Ken shoved Travis up against the wall.

There was nothing between Liz and the door. Acting on instinct, she sprang to her feet and raced out of the ice cream shop, nearly mowing down several pedestrians. The freezing air hit her in the face and stole her breath. She forced herself to run, dodging the foot

traffic on the sidewalk with no idea of where
to go.

"Hey! Liz! Stop!"

Travis's shout jabbed at her like a cattle
prod. She veered into the closest open doorway. A souvenir shop with shelves full of
Niagara Falls memorabilia. Heat encased her,
almost choking in its intensity. She skidded
to a halt at the counter where a college-aged
girl stood at the cash register looking bored.

"A phone? Do you have a phone?" Travis
still had hers in his jacket pocket.

"I'm not supposed to let customers use it,"
the girl said.

"This is an emergency." Liz saw the phone
and made a grab for it.

"Hey, what are you doing?" The girl tried
to wrest the phone from Liz's hand.

"I've got to call the police," Liz said, jerk-
ing away from the girl. She punched in 911,
thankful the emergency number was the same
in Canada as in the United States. When the
call was answered, Liz explained who she
was, that she had been kidnapped and that
she was working with ICE agent Blake Fallon and Canada Border Services officer Nathanial Longhorn. "Please contact them and
tell them I got away." She gave the woman

on the other end of the call the name of the retail shop.

"Stay put," the dispatcher said. "I'm sending patrol your way."

The sound of pounding feet on the sidewalk tore through Liz. She had to hide. She handed the phone to the girl. "Stay on the line with her."

Liz darted past the startled girl to push through the employee door. She found herself in a corridor with storage racks on either side filled with all sorts of paraphernalia. She ran for the exit at the end of the hall. She burst out of the building into an alley that stretched the length of the commercial buildings on this side of Victoria Avenue. A chain-link fence provided a barrier between the residential street and the alley. There were only two exits. Should she turn left or right?

Left would take her farther from Travis, but also farther from where Blake would be at the ice cream shop, which was to her right. She longed for his presence. With him she knew she'd be safe. Choice made. She went right, running headlong toward the end of the alley. A man stepped around the corner, blocking her path.

Ken.

He had a gun trained on her.

She came to an abrupt stop. Her feet slid on the ice and her knees protested. She nearly went down to the pavement but managed to regain her balance and stay upright.

From behind her, she heard the back door to the knickknack store bang open.

She was trapped with Ken in front of her and Travis behind her. Terrified of what might happen to her, she held up her hands and addressed Ken, "I don't have the necklace. There's no reason for you to hurt me. I don't even know where Santini is."

"Then who does have the necklace?" Ken demanded to know.

The air around Liz swirled as Travis ran to position himself between her and Ken. She stared in stunned silence at his back.

"Put the gun away," Travis said in a harsh tone that surprised Liz. "You're not going to accomplish anything with that weapon. If you kill her, there's no way we'll get the necklace back."

Liz's heart raced. She couldn't believe her new brother-in-law had stepped in front of her as a shield against Ken and his gun. Confusion swirled in her brain. Was Travis a bad guy or a good guy?

Both, she decided. Didn't everyone have the potential to do good or to do evil? It all came down to choices. Free will. A gift and a burden.

The shrill sound of sirens split the air. Ken swore a nasty streak of expletives that burned Liz's ears.

"This isn't over," Ken said. "One way or another I'm going to get those diamonds." He shoved Travis hard enough to make him fall down. Then Ken hopped over the fence and ran away, quickly disappearing.

Blake's sedan roared to a stop at the mouth of the alley. Liz ran to him. He caught her in his arms. She imprinted the feel of his embrace in her mind. His dark eyes, so full of concern, searched her face. For a moment she couldn't remember why she'd ever thought his eyes were cold when they were so rich like melted chocolate. She could dive in headfirst and never come up for air.

"Are you hurt?" he asked, his voice urgent and filled with tension.

He cared. The thought sent a ribbon of warmth to curl around her, heating her skin in a pleasant glow. "No, I'm fine. Really, I am." And she could easily stay in his embrace and be even better.

She put her cold hands to her cheeks as a way to keep herself from giving in to the need to snuggle more deeply into his arms. She was sure it was the letdown of adrenaline from being kidnapped. Certainly not anything deeper. She had to make sure of it.

To prove the point to herself, she stepped back and fought for a calm and collected demeanor. She needed to stay focused on the moment. Her sister needed her to keep a clear head and not give in to her attraction to Blake.

She pointed to the fence. "The man from the airport, Ken, escaped over the fence." She glanced back to see Nathanial once again securing Travis's hands but with metal cuffs this time. "Travis…protected me from him. He stood in front of me when Ken pointed a gun at me."

Surprise flared in Blake's eyes. A muscle jumped in his tense jaw. "That's something, I suppose."

"Travis said he purposely gave you false info on Santini's whereabouts because he doesn't think you and your team will be able to rescue Jillian. He's afraid that if Santini suspects your presence he'll kill her." A bolt of horror blazed through her as she said the last words. How would she go on if her sister died because she'd agreed to work with Blake?

Blake held her gaze. "That's not going to happen."

Though she appreciated how confident he was, she couldn't keep dread from clawing sharp talons into her. Snow began to fall, white flakes dropping from the sky to land on her uncovered head, soaking into her hair. She pulled the edges of her coat together, but nothing would stave off the chill freezing her blood.

Nathanial led Travis over. "I'll wait with him for a cruiser. You should get her out of here before the snow gets too bad."

Blake nodded. "Agreed." He turned his dark gaze on Travis. "Who's this Ken fellow? What's his connection to Santini?"

Travis shrugged. "Ken's just a two-bit thug from Miami. I've worked with him a few times when I needed to fence something. He doesn't work for Santini but he'd like to cut into Santini's business. As far as I know he's not employed by anyone."

"How does he know about the necklace?"

Liz glanced at Blake, wondering why he was asking a question that he knew the answers to.

With a grimace, Travis said, "I was spouting off. I bragged about lifting the piece. It was stupid. Stealing the necklace was stupid."

"Understatement." He cupped Liz's elbow. "Let's go."

"Wait!" Travis called. "Please, you need me to help you find Santini."

Blake left Liz's side and stalked forward to stare down Travis. "What makes you think we'd trust you again?" Blake reached into Travis's coat pocket and removed two cell phones—Liz's and the one Santini had called Travis on. "We'll find Santini without you."

A blue and white Niagara Regional Police car pulled in the alley and parked next to Blake's sedan. The two officers Travis had overpowered emerged, their expressions hard. No doubt the officers were angry at themselves for letting Travis get the upper hand. Liz had a feeling that the two officers wouldn't let it happen again. Blake greeted them, then said, "Arrest this man for kidnapping, impeding an investigation and for smuggling illegal goods."

"I'll go with them to the station," Nathanial said.

"Good." Extra protection against Travis es-

caping again. Blake turned to Liz and gestured to the sedan.

"Are you sure we don't need Travis?" Liz
said, walking fast to keep up with Blake.

"I'm sure," Blake said. "We have Santini's
number. We'll trace it and find his location,
then rescue your sister."

She climbed into his car and buckled up,
and was glad when he started the engine and
cranked up the heat. "How long will that
take?"

"I don't know," he said. "With this storm
it might take longer than I'd like." The wind-
shield wipers struggled to keep up with the
falling snow.

"Where's the necklace?"

He pulled into traffic. "In the trunk."

Seeming satisfied with that answer, she
said, "Travis wouldn't tell me where Santini
was hiding out." She couldn't keep the frustration out of her voice. "Travis is determined
to be the one to rescue Jillian since she's his
wife. But I told him he needed to let you do
your job."

Blake slanted her a glance. "I'm glad to
hear you say that."

Pleased with his approval more than she
should be, more than was smart, she set-

tled back and tried to contain herself and regain her composure. "I just don't understand Travis. He claims to love Jillian, yet he keeps putting her life in more danger."

"I've learned over the years that some people are incapable of good judgment. And some people lack common sense. Then there are those who are pure evil."

The jaded tone in his voice hurt her heart. "I'd imagine in your line of work you see a great deal of strange behaviors and horrible situations."

He nodded. "I do. Some of it is sheer stupidity. And some people buy into a lie that convinces them what they are doing is the right thing even though it makes no sense and is usually destructive."

Remembering the Sunday sermons at Peaceful Hope Church, she said, "Our pastor talked often about the battle that is constantly being waged for our souls. I suppose that's the lie you're talking about. Evil can be persuasive and pervasive."

Blake made an affirming noise in his throat. "That's true."

When the sedan slowed, Liz realized they were in line to cross the Rainbow Bridge back into the United States. She sat up straight. "What are we doing? Why are we leaving Canada?"

"I need you to go home so I can do my job without having to worry about you, too," he said in an exceptionally even tone that grated on her nerves.

"No way," she said, setting her jaw. "I'm not leaving."

"Yes, you are."

Desperation crawled through her. "You can't force me onto a plane, and the second you leave, I'll head back to Canada."

"Not if you're stopped at the border."

Her stomach dropped. He'd do that? Put her name on some watch list so the border agents wouldn't let her cross? How could he so calmly send her away when he knew how much seeing her sister rescued meant to her? She opened the car door.

"Liz!"

She jumped out of the slow-moving vehicle. She had to jog a few steps to keep from taking a headlong splat into the snow-covered curb. She wasn't sure where she dredged up the courage or the gumption to not only defy him but to brazenly exit a moving car, but the sense of empowerment surging through her was like nothing she'd ever felt before.

The sedan screeched to a halt. The car behind them blared its horn as Blake climbed out of the car and stalked to her. "Are you insane? You don't jump out of a moving car. You could've been injured."

"The car was barely crawling and I'm fine." She crossed her arms over her chest to keep from showing how freaked-out she was. She'd never done anything like that before. Impulsiveness was Jillian's way, not hers. She thought things through, approached life in a methodical and careful way. However, she'd never faced a situation like this before. In the course of forty-eight hours she'd not only left her island home, she'd also teamed up with law enforcement and been kidnapped by her brother-in-law. And now she had jumped out of a moving vehicle!

Her life was spinning out of her control.

But she wouldn't let him see how out of her element she was. She lifted her chin and faced Blake with determination. "Blake, you can't send me home without Jillian."

He scrubbed a hand over his jaw. "You're a distraction, Liz. I need to keep my focus on Santini if I'm going to bring your sister home to you safely."

She tucked away his admission that he was

distracted by her and concentrated on her objective—to convince him to let her stay and help. Her sister needed her. "I've done everything you've asked. I had no control over Travis kidnapping me, and I managed to escape on my own. I promise I'll stay out of the way. But I can't leave here without Jillian."

He shook his head. "Liz, it's—"

She held up a hand. "Do you have a sibling? A sister?"

He frowned. "My having a sister has nothing to do with what's going on here."

"Yes, it does," she insisted, needing him to see this from her perspective. "If your sister had been taken hostage, you'd do anything for her, right? You'd want to be here when she was rescued. You'd want to make sure everyone was doing everything they could to bring her home safely."

"I'd trust the authorities whose job it was to bring her home," he countered.

"It isn't a matter of trust. I know you'll do your job." She needed him to understand. "I'm not asking to be involved. All I want is to stay in Niagara until you've rescued my sister. She's all the family I have left. I would go nuts sitting alone at home waiting for word."

Indecision warred on his face.

SIX

A fat tear rolled down Liz's cheek to mingle with the crystal flakes landing with abandon on her pale skin. The sight scored Blake to the quick. He hated to see her tears, knowing he caused them. He reached up to caress her cheek, wiping away a tear with his thumb.

The snow fell in earnest now, blanketing the cars queued up at the border crossing in white as if somehow the purity of the flakes could cover the harsh reality that faced them.

Liz's question about what he'd do if it were his sister who had been kidnapped struck deep. There was no way for Liz to know he hadn't seen his little sister in nearly a decade. They'd been torn apart when their parents divorced. She'd gone with their mother, while he'd stayed with his father.

He'd only seen his sister, Emily, a handful of times after that, and now as an adult she lived in Australia with her husband and two kids. She'd left the United States on her eighteenth birthday and never looked back. Christmas cards and pictures were the only communication Blake had with Emily and her family.

However, Liz was right. If Emily were in danger, if she'd been kidnapped and held for ransom, he'd move mountains and whatever other obstacles stood in his way to rescue her. But he was an officer of the law, not a civilian.

He understood Liz's need to stay close by. How could he deny her that much at least? He couldn't. He'd just have to find a way to keep his focus on capturing Santini. He couldn't let Liz distract him from that goal, but he could allow her to remain in town.

A Canadian border patrol officer ran over. "Is there a problem here?"

With a sigh, Blake showed the man his badge. "No problem."

"You can't leave your vehicle in the middle of the lane," the officer said. "We've got to keep the cars moving before the snow makes driving impossible."

"We were just leaving," Blake replied. He

held out his hand to Liz. "We're heading back into Niagara."

Her eyes lit up, and she put her hand in his. Her skin was as cold as ice. He tucked her hand into the crook of his arm and hustled her back to the sedan. Once he had her safely inside, he climbed in and turned the heat on full blast. He made a U-turn and headed back into the city.

"Thank you," she said in a soft voice.

His heart contracted, showing him just how much she did affect him. Her courage and determination were worthy of his respect and admiration. Her vulnerability, that she tried so hard to hide, endeared her to him in a way he'd never experienced before and wasn't sure he liked. She made him feel emotions that he'd rather not deal with. "You have to keep your promise that you'll stay out of the way and do as I ask."

When she didn't respond, he glanced over to see her biting on her lower lip. A moment of misgiving tore at him. "Liz. Promise me."

She faced him and nodded. "I'll do my best to keep my promise."

Not exactly what he'd wanted but it was probably the best he'd get. He groaned and prayed he didn't live to regret this decision.

Wind buffeted the sedan, rattling the windows. The storm was in full swing. He had to concentrate on the road. The painted lines had disappeared beneath inches of snowfall. The going was slow and arduous.

His cell phone rang. He answered, putting it on speaker so he could keep his hands on the steering wheel. "Fallon."

"Where are you?" Drew asked.

"Heading back to the condo with Liz. I have you on speakerphone."

"Ah. We're headed back, too. But we're in a horrible traffic jam."

"It's not much better where we are," he said, braking to avoid hitting the bumper of the minivan ahead of him when the van stopped abruptly.

"We were able to get an address where Santini called Travis from," Drew said. "He's holed up in a house on the outskirts of town. At least he was when he made the call."

"Good." Blake looked at Liz. He could see the worry on her pretty face. "Then hopefully that means Jillian is someplace warm and dry."

"Yes. We were headed there, but we had to turn back because of road closures."

"It's doubtful Santini will be going any-where in this storm," Blake said.

"True, might be a good time to pay him a visit though, eh?"

"Santini wouldn't expect a raid in the middle of a whiteout," Blake agreed.

"When I get back to the condo I'll coordinate with the Niagara Regional Police."

"We'll see what we can do about getting outfitted for the snow," Drew said. "Sami says to text her your sizes for boots, pants and jacket."

"Will do. See you soon." Blake clicked off.

Seeing a public parking garage, he turned in. "It'll be faster if we hoof it the last few blocks. Are you up for the hike?"

"I'm used to storms, though I will say I wish I had my snow boots," Liz said.

He marveled at her resilience. This woman was so much more than he'd first thought. She was slowly wiggling her way into his heart against his will. And he didn't know what to do about it. "I've never owned snow boots," he said as he parked and texted Sami the info she'd requested. "Not much use for them in Alabama where I grew up or in Seattle where I now call home."

She smiled as she climbed out of the car.

"I was right. You're from the south. Where in Alabama?"

"Pelham." He opened the trunk and grabbed the bag with the necklace inside. He rolled it up to fit into his coat pocket. "It's a small community about twenty minutes south of Birmingham."

Tucking her closer to keep them both warm, they hurried out of the three-story parking garage. A few other brave pedestrians hustled by. She fit so well against him.

"Is your family still there?" she asked, though her voice was muffled as she turned into him and huddled against the onslaught of freezing flakes that dampened her hair and jacket.

Despite the cold he started to grow warm. It was a struggle to concentrate. "My dad. He's retired now, but he was the chief of police."

"Ah, so law enforcement is in your blood. What about your mom?"

"She and Dad divorced when I was ten." The sidewalk was slippery beneath their feet. He held on tight to Liz. "She took my little sister and moved to Chicago."

"That must have been hard for you and your dad," she murmured on a shiver.

In so many ways. Up ahead, he could see the tall brick building like a beacon, guiding them through the snow. His feet were numb from the cold and his pant legs wet. Car horns blared. Tires spun. The street had become icy. A small pickup truck slid, its tires throwing up debris as it tried to grip the pavement.

The sensation of being scrutinized itched at the nape of his neck. He glanced around at the other pedestrians with bowed heads in deference to the icy snow, coats and jackets zipped to the chin. No one seemed to pay them any special attention. Yet he couldn't shake the feeling that someone, somewhere, was watching as he and Liz hurried along the wide sidewalk with the goal of a warm condo for their effort.

They reached the end of the sidewalk. The condo building was across the side street. Instead of crossing the street when the light turned green, Blake urged Liz inside the corner market. The heated interior made his numb ears thaw and tingle.

"How about we pick up some supplies?" he asked to cover the real reason for the stop.

Though she gave him a curious look, she said, "Sure. Like what?"

"Coffee. I think we're low." He kept his

gaze out the picture window. "And soup. Maybe some bread. Whatever you want."

Liz moved away to gather his requested items. Blake stepped closer to the window. Through the thick, falling snow he could barely make out a tall man wearing a pea coat and fedora standing across the wide expanse of the main street. The guy from the airport had had a fedora and pea coat on. What had the informant said his name was? Ken. That's right. He wanted Santini's necklace. Not going to happen. Blake's initial instinct was to rush out and apprehend the man, but Liz's safety came first. He needed to stay with her.

Blake turned to the cashier, a buxom brunette who eyed him as if he was her favorite candy dish.

"Anything I can do for you?" she asked in a sultry tone. "Anything at all."

Ignoring her blatant attempt to flirt with him, he showed her his badge. "Is there a back exit?"

She gestured toward the far left corner of the store. "End of the dairy aisle through the gray flaps. I could show you if you'd like."

Liz stepped up then with a basketful of goods. Her gaze bounced between him and the brunette behind the counter but she didn't say a word.

"That won't be necessary." He paid for the groceries, then hefted the bag in one arm and snagged Liz's elbow with the other to prevent her from stepping out the front entrance. "This way."

"What's happened?" she asked, her voice slightly high with anxiety.

"That Ken guy is outside."

She twisted to look over her shoulder. "He had a gun."

"He must have doubled back and followed us." He pushed aside the long flaps suspended from the top of the doorway. They entered the storage area. Before they left the store through the back exit, Blake called the Niagara Regional Police office and reported Ken's location. "He's armed and dangerous," Blake added.

He hung up and pushed open the back door. Outside, the raging blizzard had intensified. Tucking Liz into his side, he ducked his head and they tramped out into the wall of white toward the condo. They hustled the short half block to the building's side entrance. He used his key card to open the glass doors and they hurried inside. He made sure the door shut and locked behind him. They stomped the snow from their shoes. Blake's feet were numb from the cold. As they rode the elevator up, feeling returned to his extremities with pins and needles.

They reached the condo just as the electricity went out, plunging them into gloom. The curtains of the large picture window allowed light that penetrated the wall of white outside to illuminate the condo, so they weren't in total darkness.

Blake set the groceries on the dining table. He removed the bag containing the jewelry box with the diamond necklace from his coat pocket, then shrugged out of his wet overcoat and hung it up in the laundry room. Liz followed him and hung her coat up, as well.

"There are flashlights in the entryway closet," he said as they moved back to the entryway.

"We'll need those if the lights don't come back on before nightfall." She headed for the hall. "I'm going to change clothes. I'll be right back."

Needing to do the same, Blake headed to his room where he traded his soggy pants for dry and warm sweatpants. Then he called Nathanial.

"Hey," Nathanial greeted him. "Where are you?"

"We're back at the condo. You?"

"We? Did Drew and Sami make it there?"

Blake grimaced. "Not yet. I've got Liz here."

There was a slight pause before Nathanial said, "Interesting."

A slight note of amusement laced the word. Blake scrubbed a hand over his face. "Yeah. I'm a sap. I let her talk me out of taking her back to the US."

Nathanial barked out a laugh. "It's good to know your cold heart can be thawed."

"Cute," Blake shot back. "Is Travis in custody?"

"He is. I'm sticking around until the storm lessens," Nathanial said. "I figure I'll take another run at Travis and see if there's more he could tell us about Santini's operation."

"Good idea. Have you heard from Drew?"

"Not in a while."

"Okay. Keep me posted if you get anything from Travis."

"Will do. And Blake…"

"Yes?"

"It's okay for you to have feelings for Liz. It wouldn't be the end of the world if you fell for her. Who knows? She may be just what you need."

Blake's gut clenched. He didn't do romance. He didn't do serious. Especially not with someone involved in a case. That was a perilous path. Once he had Santini in custody and Liz's sister safely home, Blake would move on to his next assignment, which meant he couldn't have, didn't want or need, ties to anyone or any place.

Deciding the best course of action was not to acknowledge his friend's remark, he said, "I'll talk to you later."

Nathanial snorted. "Sure, whatever you say, eh?"

Shaking his head, Blake clicked off, shoving Nathaniel's comment to the furthest reaches of his mind. Then Blake called Niagara Regional Police to coordinate a raid on Santini. He also asked for a female officer to come to the condo to stay with Liz while they took down Santini and rescued her sister. After he hung up, he went in search of Liz. She had lit several votive candles, lighting the place in a soft glow. He stopped to light the gas fireplace, which provided warmth and more light.

Clanking pots and pans drew him to the kitchen. She had opened a can of soup and had it simmering on the gas stove. She now stood at the counter, chopping veggies for a salad. Her honey-blond hair was swept up in a messy bun exposing the creamy white column of her neck. She'd changed into casual athletic wear with a matching pullover. His gaze raked over her feminine form before lifting to meet her sea-green eyes. An invisible current of attraction drew him closer. If he got too close, would he get burned?

"Can I help?" he asked, his voice coming out huskier than he'd have liked.

She gave a tiny nod. "You could melt some butter for the bread."

A grin tugged at the corner of his mouth. The way he was feeling with her so close he could melt the butter with his hands. "Sure, I can do that."

He was surprised by how comfortable and relaxing it was to work side by side with her. When they finished the preparations, they took their meal to the dining table.

"Drew and Sami should be here soon,"

Blake said as they took their meal to the dining table.

"There's certainly plenty of food."

"We'll be heading out not long after they arrive."

"Good." She set down her fork. "I'm worried about Jillian. I just want this nightmare over."

"That's understandable."

"But I have to trust God will keep her safe until she's rescued."

Unnerved by her words and the sentiment behind them, he said, "Can you really do that? Trust Him? Aren't you angry that He allowed your sister to be put in harm's way to begin with?"

Her brow furrowed. "I don't blame God for somebody else's actions."

"You're much more magnanimous than I am," he said. He couldn't help the anger that simmered deep in his gut over Liam's death. "My friend Liam was a man of faith. He helped me see the need to believe in something greater than myself, yet God allowed Liam to die. Faith didn't protect him."

Liz reached across the table to cover his clenched fist. He concentrated on the feel of her warm and soft skin against his hand to keep from giving in to the sorrow that lurked at the edges of his mind. "We all die at some point. Some too soon in life." She frowned. "I pray it's not Jillian's time."

Liz had felt the bite of death in her life with the loss of both of her parents. And now her sister's life hung in the balance. Blake couldn't imagine the grief Liz must carry. He relaxed his fingers and turned his hand over so their palms met. "I'm sorry. That was insensitive of me."

A sad smile tipped up the edges of her mouth. "Believe me, I've done my share of blaming God, asking Him why my parents had to die. Even wondering why Jillian has been put in danger. But the unfortunate fact is that humanity comes with sickness and evil and accidents and death. Turning my back on God would mean my connection with Him was conditional. And that would be very sad, because if God's love came with conditions…" She shook her head.

"But doesn't it? The Ten Commandments and all that?"

"I'm not saying there aren't instructions and principles that we should live by." She paused as if searching for how to explain. "Think of it this way, most parents love their children unconditionally. When their child messes up, the parent corrects, guides and chastises but they still love their child. That's how God is with us. He's about relationships, whereas most humans, outside of parental love, are relational."

He thought about all the times he rebelled or lashed out at his parents. Especially when he was a teenager so full of anger at them both for tearing their family apart. And yet, no matter how nasty his behavior, he hadn't doubted his dad's love or his mother's. Though Dad didn't show his love with hugs and kisses, he'd made time for Blake, taking days off to spend with him fishing and catching a baseball game. Mom had loved him, too, and continually told him he could come live with her and Emily. But he'd chosen to stay with his dad.

On one of his last assignments, he and Nathanial had provided backup to DEA agent Tyler Griffin by going undercover on a Christmas-tree farm in northern Idaho. The widow who owned the farm had a young son, and though Blake hadn't had much experience with kids, he'd had a soft spot for the little guy. Tyler had ended up marrying the widow and Blake regularly checked in on them and their son. "Okay, I kind of get the parental love thing. But you lost me on the last part."

"I guess what I'm saying is we, meaning humans, put conditions on our relationships, and when one of the two parties in the relationship does something that fractures the connection, it's too easy to give up and walk away or strike out at the other person. Then that person retaliates by striking out or giving up and walking away."

"Like my parents," Blake murmured. How many nights had he lain awake hearing them fighting until finally his mother had walked away, leaving both him and his father behind? And wasn't he just as guilty? After catching his college girlfriend, Sarah, in several lies, he'd washed his hands of the relationship. No second chances.

In fact, he'd not allowed a deep relationship since because he didn't want to be hurt again. He didn't want to be weak.

But what would have happened had he chosen to love unconditionally? Would he and Sarah still be together? What path would his life have taken if he'd elected to work through the pain and allowed her to regain his trust? What life would his father have had if he'd allowed himself to fully love his wife rather than shut her out?

The questions ricocheted through his mind. He wasn't one to contemplate "what if's." He stayed in the moment, taking life as it came and letting the past go.

A mocking laugh in his head belied that thought, making him aware he hadn't truly let go of the past. If he had, then maybe he wouldn't be alone.

He frowned at the idea. He wanted to be alone. He liked not having someone tying him down to one place.

Liz squeezed his hand drawing his attention. "Now I'm the one being insensitive."

"No. You're right. It is too easy to give up on God—or others—when things get tough and painful." But it was hard for him to think that God could love him as flawed as he was. Could he have a closer relationship, a real relationship with God?

Staring into Liz's pretty eyes, he found himself yearning for a relationship with her. A real give and take. The kind that lasted a lifetime. His heart pounded in his chest and a suffocating swell of emotion threatened to drown him. Did he really want a relationship with this woman?

Right now, this minute, the possibility held him enthralled. He had to admit he found Liz Cantrell challenging and exciting. He respected her drive and her loyalty to her sister. She had a fierce, determined nature that was tempered by a gentle side he found alluring. She held him captive in ways he'd never experienced. What did that mean? What did he want it to mean?

"You sound as if you speak from experience."

Her soft voice broke through his thoughts like a hammer against concrete, shattering the moment. "Yes. Though in retrospect I was the one who failed. Failed to love unconditionally. I'm not sure I'm capable of doing so."

"If it were easy…" She shrugged. "Whatever happened, it's in the past, right?" She chewed on her bottom lip. He had the feeling her words were having as much of an impact on her as they were on him.

He'd let the past cloud his choices. The knowledge disturbed him in ways he'd rather not feel.

He slipped his hand from hers and picked up his empty bowl and plate and carried them to the sink. She followed with her dishes. He turned on the faucet, thankful that water hadn't gone off like the electricity. As he handwashed their dishes, Liz grabbed a towel and dried.

"I'm sorry if I upset you," she said.

"Not at all." He scrubbed a bowl with more vigor than needed.

"It's okay if you don't want to talk about it," she said. "We all have painful times in our pasts."

That made him curious. He turned to face her and leaned his hip against the counter. "What painful secrets are you hiding?"

She tucked in her chin. "Nothing you'd be interested in."

"I am, though." He lifted her chin with the crook of his finger. He wanted to know more about this woman, despite knowing nothing good would come from getting emotionally involved with her. Yet he couldn't make himself shut down his curiosity or his attraction to her.

He flashed back to Tyler and to the words Blake had said to him when it had become clear Tyler was getting in too deep with the widow who had owned the Christmas-tree farm.

Someone's gonna get hurt. They always do.

Good advice he should heed. He went back to scrubbing dishes.

Before he could retract his words, she spoke. "My second year of college I fell head over heels for a guy in my econ class. Joe. He was very charismatic, and I was over the moon that he was paying attention to me to the point he was all I could think about. I couldn't stand to be apart from him and my grades slipped."

She let out a dry laugh. "Then Jillian pointed out I was just like Dad. Putting everything into this one person." She put the clean dishes back in the cupboard. "That's what our father did. He had no real identity apart from Mom, and didn't want any. So when she died he was beyond devastated. He didn't know who he was or how to live without her."

"But isn't that how love is supposed to go?"

"No, love wants the best for the other person. Losing my identity to Joe wasn't love. It was more of an obsession. Then when I broke up with him, he became obsessed with me and finally backed off when my godfather, Sheriff Ward, had a talk with him." She shrugged. "Since then I haven't wanted to get close to anyone for fear of losing myself."

"It's a blessing you had the sheriff in your corner."

"Yes, Sheriff Ward has been a blessing to our family."

It was good to know she was as leery as he was of anything deeper than what they already had, though he wasn't sure what to call what they had. He wasn't really her bodyguard, nor her jailer.

Yet, he'd take a bullet meant for her without thought. He liked to think he would for anyone—his job was to protect, after all—but somehow the thought of Liz in peril tore him up inside.

He reached for her before he thought better of it. She came willingly into his arms. She was so slight and delicate, he was almost afraid of holding her too tightly.

She reached up to trace the line of his jaw with her soft, gentle fingers. "Who hurt you?"

His first inclination was to deny answering, but for some reason he wanted to open up to this woman. "I was engaged once years ago."

Liz held still in his arms, her gaze never wavering.

"We were a few months away from the

big day when I discovered she'd been lying to me about so many things." He shook his head. "Stupid things, too. Like spending more money on clothes than she'd admitted. We weren't married so what did it matter how much she spent? Yet she'd make a big show of saying she spent only so much money, then asking to borrow money from me because she couldn't pay her Visa bill. Of course I helped her out but when I saw the bill I realized she'd fabricated how much she'd actually spent. And then she'd lie about where she was or where she was going. She'd lie about who she was with. That hurt the worst. I finally had to realize and come to terms with the fact she was a habitual liar. But she didn't see it as an issue. I did."

"She didn't want to get help?"

"No, she said it was my problem, that I couldn't accept her as she was," he shrugged. "She was right. I couldn't. Not like that. So I broke it off."

"That's understandable." Liz laid her hand over his heart. "It would be hard to marry someone who you could never fully trust."

He liked that she understood. "Yes, that's exactly it."

She peered up at him, her eyes guileless and searching. "Trust is important to you."

Wariness invaded him. "It is. Very much so."

A tiny smile lifted the corners of her lips. "You're a very good man, Agent Blake Fallon."

The wariness seeped away to be replaced with yearning. He wasn't sure that her statement was true about him, but he was definitely sure he wanted to kiss her right now.

His thought must have shown on his face because her lips parted in invitation. He nearly groaned. Did she even understand what she did to him? How irresistible he found her?

Slowly, he lowered his head just as the sound of the front door opening froze him in place a mere fraction from her delectable mouth.

Drew and Sami entered the condo. Face heating, he stepped back, his relief at not having given in to the uninvited yearning matched by the relief on Liz's face. They'd almost let the situation take a turn neither of them wanted to take. Clearly they were in agreement.

That should be a good thing, right? So why

did he feel as if he'd missed an opportunity that might never come again? Why did he still want to know so much more about her? Why did his mouth still crave the chance to touch hers?

SEVEN

Liz moved away from Blake, grateful to see Sami and Drew entering the condo. With each step putting distance between her and him, she breathed easier. She'd nearly let Blake kiss her. And she'd wanted him to. With everything in her she'd longed for his kiss. Wow, where was her head? She forced her attraction to Blake to the farthest reaches of her heart.

It was bad enough she'd told him about Joe. For years she'd refused to entertain thoughts of that part of her past because she was embarrassed by the way she'd acted, by the fact that she'd lost herself even if it had been for a short period of time.

She didn't want to be that person ever again. If she ever decided to give her heart for a second time, she would go slow and be methodical about her choice. Which meant she had to resist the temptation to fall for Agent Fallon. Their lives had intersected for this short period of time, but their paths would diverge as soon as Jillian was free and Santini in jail. There was no future for them.

But what if there could be? A little voice inside her head asked. Her pulse skipped a beat at the question.

She didn't have an answer, wasn't even sure she wanted to let her mind go there. Blake had a power and charisma about him that scared her and yet at the same time drew her to him. Best not to contemplate something as dangerous as a life that included Blake, despite how much she was coming to respect and admire him.

Liz helped Sami off with her coat. "You two must be famished. There are several cans of soup in the pantry and all the fixings for a salad that need to be eaten before they go bad."

Sami grinned. "Wonderful. I'm starved. We haven't eaten since breakfast." She shivered. "But first I need to change into dry clothes. It's freezing out there."

Drew set a large bag on the floor. "We found a sporting goods store, but they didn't have everything we needed."

Blake stepped up behind Liz. Awareness shimmied up her spine. He was so close she could smell his aftershave. The woodsy scent had teased her all day. She glanced at him, noting the darkening of stubble marking his jawline. Some men needed the scruffy look to strengthen their jaw, but not Blake. With or without the shadow of a beard, strength was inherent in his face, his demeanor. He was a man other men envied and women fawned over, like the cashier at the convenience store had.

Though Liz knew better, she longed to reach up and run her hand over the angles and contours of his handsome face. Instead, she shoved her fists into the pocket of her zipped-up sweat jacket, the soft material doing nothing to alleviate her yearning to feel the roughness of his beard against her palms.

She needed something to do before she broke down and gave in to her attraction to Blake. "I'll put on the soup."

She retreated into the kitchen while Blake and Drew moved into the living room. The tension in her chest eased. She really needed to get a grip and keep control of her emotions. Especially when it came to Blake. She'd never had this problem before. None of the men she'd dated after Joe had made her heart race and her common sense desert her, the way Blake did. And that scared her.

"We'll need to hold off on raiding Santini's lair until the storm subsides," Drew stated. "There's no going anywhere in this blizzard. It's a mess out there. We barely made it here. We had to trudge the last few blocks on foot."

"Same here. And if that's true for us then it has to be true for Santini," Blake said. "I'd still like to get eyes on the house. I'll contact Nathanial and see what he can do."

Blake disappeared down the hall. Drew warmed his hands at the gas fireplace. Liz turned the burner on simmer and walked into the living room. "Do you believe my sister is safe?"

Drew lifted his gaze to her. "I do. Santini's no fool. He's greedy. If anything happens to her, he'll never get his diamonds, and that's what matters to him. Money is his motivator."

She was glad to hear him say essentially the same thing Blake had told her back in the airport interrogation room. Though only forty-eight hours had passed since the day she'd walked off the plane and had been stopped by Blake and Nathanial, it seemed as if all of that had occurred a lifetime ago. She had a hard time visualizing what it would be like to return home and to never see Blake again. A strange hollowness invaded her, making her ache deep inside.

But once Jillian was safe, Liz would return home and go back to the life she'd made for herself in South Carolina. Why she was having to remind herself of that she couldn't fathom. It wasn't as if Blake had declared his undying love for her. Yeah, so he'd almost kissed her, but that didn't mean anything more than he felt the same pull of attraction.

The fact they'd exchanged their past hurts only meant that…well, she really didn't know what it meant. She wouldn't let it mean anything.

When Blake returned to the living room she had a hard time not moving to his side.

"Nathanial's going to do recon on Santini's house," Blake informed them.

"Won't it be dangerous for him to be out in this storm?" Liz asked. Why would anyone want to brave a whiteout like the one raging outside the window?

"He was born and raised in this type of weather," Blake replied, his gaze bouncing to her and then away.

Still, she worried about the Canadian officer. "Should he go alone?"

"Nathanial is a bit of a lone wolf," Drew commented. "I'm sure he'd rather not have company. He can move faster on his own."

That made sense in some ways, but if anything went wrong, he'd have no safety net. She sent up a silent prayer for his safety. "How long have you worked with Blake and Nathanial?"

Drew shot Blake a grin. "Blake, a year or so. However, Nathanial and I have been acquaintances for several years. He's as solid as they come. But he certainly has a way with the ladies."

Blake made a noise in his throat. "You got that right."

Drew nodded with a lopsided smile. "I'm just glad Sami met me first."

Liz couldn't imagine Sami falling for anyone but Drew. The two seemed so well matched. "Does Nathanial have a family? A wife?"

"No, he's the quintessential bachelor," Drew informed her. "The woman who tames him will have to be someone extremely special with a strong personality to see past his charm to the real man who would lay down his life for any one of us in a heartbeat."

She wanted to ask if Blake was the same way. She slanted him a glance. Would it take someone special to tame him? Was she special enough? The wayward thought locked her tongue to the roof of her mouth.

Liz was grateful when Sami joined them dressed in comfortable yoga pants and a tunic sweatshirt. Liz took the opportunity to return to the kitchen on the pretext of removing the soup from the burner.

"Thank you," Sami said as she followed her into the kitchen. "You don't have to wait on us."

"I know," Liz said. "But it helps me to have something to do while we wait." She began chopping more veggies for their salad. Keeping her hands busy kept her from thinking too much about Blake. "I can't help but worry about Jillian. If something happens to her…" She couldn't stop the burn of tears at the back of her throat.

Sami rubbed a hand on Liz's shoulder. "You have to stay positive. Have some faith in us. We know what we're doing."

"I keep praying for her. For all of us." Though Blake was high on her list.

"Prayer is good. God will see us through this. He'll see you and Jillian through this."

Knowing Sami believed in God warmed Liz's heart. "Thank you for saying that. You're right, I have to stop imagining the worst." But how did she control her imaginings?

The sound of a phone ringing echoed off the condo's high ceilings.

Blake walked into the kitchen with Liz's ringing cell phone in his hand. He held the call display up for her to see. "It's Jillian calling."

An anxious flurry spread through her, cooling her blood and making her palms sweat. "Maybe she escaped?"

The doubt on Blake's face didn't require him to answer.

"It's most likely Santini. I'll put it on speaker," Blake said, then depressed the answer button and then the speaker button. He nodded to Liz.

Her mouth went dry and her voice deserted her for a moment. Finally, she managed to squawk out a "Hello."

"Lizzie," Jillian's shaky voice filled the kitchen.

Liz grabbed the phone from Blake but left it on speaker. "Jillian, are you okay?"

"Yes. But he wants the necklace or he'll—" She let out a sob. "Lizzie, he'll kill me."

The weight of responsibility pressed down on Liz's chest, making her heart heavy with panic. "I'll give it to him. But the storm—"

"Will be gone by tomorrow." Santini's voice came over the line. Apparently he'd taken the phone away from Jillian. "We'll try this again. And this is your last chance. Bring the necklace to Queen Victoria Park at ten p.m. tomorrow night. I know you've brought the cops in. But they better not show up tomorrow or your sister will take a nosedive off the top of the falls." He hung up.

An uncontrollable tremor made Liz drop the phone. It clattered on the hardwood floor. The mental image of her sister falling into the freezing waters of the Niagara River made Liz dizzy with fear. Her lungs refused to draw in air.

Blake gripped her by the shoulders, his big hands warm and comforting. "Hold it together, Liz. Nothing is going to happen to Jillian."

"He knows about you," she said, her voice not much more than a whisper. She gasped for breath. Would her worst nightmare come true?

"He does, and he hasn't hurt your sister,"

Blake pointed out. He slowly rubbed his hands up and down her arms. "That's good news. He wants the necklace more than he wants to shed blood."

She needed to believe his words, but the worst-case scenario thinking that seemed so ingrained into her psyche wouldn't relent. She pictured her sister's body plunging into the frozen river, breaking through the ice and plummeting to the bottom.

Blake gave her a gentle shake. "Stay with me, Liz. You can't let the fear win. I need you to be strong and ready to be reunited with your sister."

Staring into his obsidian eyes, she saw her pale reflection, but she also saw concern and care. She planted her palms on his chest and felt the steady rhythm of his heartbeat. He made her want to be strong, made her want to rise above the terror threatening to drag her down into despair. For Jillian, Liz would do anything—even face this ordeal with bravery.

With effort she filled her lungs with oxygen, clearing her head and infusing courage into every fiber of her being. She inclined her head. "I can do this."

Blake tipped his head down slightly to capture her gaze. "You're not doing anything other than staying out of the way."

She arched her eyebrows. "Excuse me? Didn't you just tell me I had to be strong?"

"And you do. The last thing we need is you falling apart now."

She stepped back, out of his reach. "I'm not going to fall apart. I'm taking the necklace to the park tomorrow night."

The thunderclouds in Blake's dark eyes rivaled the raging storm outside. "No way."

"Yes, way." She looked to Sami and Drew for help. They regarded her with a mix of respect and concern. "What do you two think?"

Drew shrugged and looked at Blake. "I'm inclined to let her make the exchange."

"Me, too," Sami piped in. "She's proven she can handle herself. If Santini sees anyone other than her there, he may follow through with his threat and then flee. This is our best opportunity to catch him."

"And if he sends one of his minions again?" Blake ground out. "I say we raid the house the minute the storm breaks enough for us to leave here."

Drew nodded. "Agreed. That's our first option."

"The only option," Blake stated in a flat voice. "I will not put Liz in any more danger."

Though a part of Liz appreciated his concern for her well-being, she wouldn't let him control her. No one controlled her. "That's not your choice to make."

Blake glowered at her. "This is my operation, my call."

Liz fisted her hands on her hips. "Not if I walk out that door."

"Go ahead," he called her bluff. "But the necklace remains with us. It's evidence. Then what, Liz? What will you have to bargain with?"

Annoyance crowded her chest. But she had to grab her temper by the edges and keep it from flying loose. Fighting with him wouldn't get her very far. "Do your raid. If that fails, then you let me do what I have to in order to save my sister."

That he wanted to argue with her was clear in the way his upper lip drew back. But she wasn't afraid of him or his anger. One thing she knew as truth was Agent Blake Fallon was a man of honor and integrity. Any doubts she'd had to the contrary were long gone. She held her ground and his gaze. He clamped his teeth together so tight a muscle jumped in his jaw. She doubted he'd appreciate it if she suggested he get a bite guard for times like this.

"We raid," he finally said in a tight voice. "If Santini gets past our net, then we'll discuss the drop at Queen Victoria Park."

Knowing that was the best she'd get from him, she nodded with a grateful smile. "Thank you."

"Don't thank me until we have your sister in our custody," he said before turning on his heels and leaving the kitchen.

An awkward silence remained in his wake.

Liz squared her shoulders and lifted her chin. She forced a smile for Sami and Drew. "I'll say good-night, then."

She headed to her room but couldn't shake the sinking feeling in the pit of her stomach. She didn't like having Blake angry with her. But more than that she didn't like that she cared.

The next morning, Liz awoke from a fitful sleep just as night faded and the first rays of sunrise glistened off the crystalized flakes of snow piled high all over the city. From her bedroom window Liz could see the frozen falls, and despite the mild warmth of the sun streaming through the window, she shivered as Santini's threat echoed through her mind.

She knelt and prayed this would end today. That Blake and his team would successfully bring Santini and his thugs to justice while rescuing her sister. And then she wouldn't see Blake again. A curious emptiness filled her. It would be hard to say goodbye to the handsome agent. Only because they'd been in such close proximity these past few days. She'd get used to not having him around quick enough. Wouldn't she?

A light knock on the door brought her to her feet. She opened the door to find Blake on the other side. He'd shaved, his smooth jaw even more enticing than his stubbled one had been last night. She breathed in his woodsy aftershave, imprinting the scent on her brain. His dark hair was blow-dried into a tousled look that worked on him. He was dressed in a white snowsuit.

Her white knight off to rescue her sister.

"Good morning." His deep voice wrapped around her like a comfortable blanket.

"Good morning." She managed to keep her voice even and not betray the inner flutter of attraction that always hovered at the edges of her consciousness. "I see you're ready to go after Santini."

"Yes. We're heading out," he replied in a measured tone as if he were afraid she'd demand to accompany them.

She did want to go but understood that she'd be more of a hindrance than a help. She needed him focused on Jillian. She saw the validity in his view that she could be a potential distraction. "I pray you succeed."

"We will." His confidence was reassuring. "Officer Fordham of the Niagara Regional Police is here to keep you company."

She appreciated his attempt to soften the fact that the officer was there to guard her. Or was it to keep her from leaving?

"Where's the necklace?" she asked.

"In a safe place."

He didn't trust her with it? "You'll let me know the minute you have Jillian?"

"Of course." He cupped her cheek, his hand warm against her skin. "Trust me, Liz. We'll bring your sister back safely."

"From your lips to God's ears," she murmured, relishing his touch. When his hand dropped away, she almost whimpered. How long had it been since she'd allowed anyone close enough to touch her so tenderly? Longer than she'd cared to admit. The craving for more of his touch, for more of the easy companionship they'd shared the night before, clawed through her, shredding the walls she'd built up to protect herself.

Not good. Not good at all. She couldn't let herself fall for this man even though she realized, with a sense of impending dread, that there was a part of her heart that beat a little too fast when he was near.

She needed some distance. She needed to return to her quiet uneventful life on her island home. Unfortunately, she had a feeling that leaving Blake behind would be harder than she'd expected. Or wanted.

Blake lay on a snow mound with a military-grade, heat-sensing, thermal-imaging camera pointed at the boxy house situated on an acre piece of land that was blanketed in ice-crusted snow. He saw no heat signatures. Nothing. The house appeared empty. Or Santini had installed some sort of thermal imagining block. "Are we sure they're still in there?"

Beside him, Nathanial snorted. "No. There's been no movement since I arrived at midnight. They could have braved the elements and vacated before I got here. Or the house is set up with technology to prevent detection."

"I wouldn't put it past Santini to have his lair fitted with Mylar," Blake said.

"Now, that'd be something, eh?" Nathanial shifted. "I say we breech."

Blake slowly swung the camera over the area, picking up the heat signatures of the Niagara Regional Police officers dressed in tactical gear who were scattered in various hiding spots and waiting for the signal to go in. Drew and Sami also waited in the shadow of a tree grove.

He said a quick prayer for safety. There was risk involved. They all knew it, but hoped this would go off without anyone being injured. "Okay, give the signal."

Blake rolled over onto his back to stuff the camera into his duffle and then checked his weapon.

Nathanial spoke into his communication link. "It's a go. Proceed with caution. We have one hostage to extract by any means."

Blake flipped back to his stomach. A wide stretch of exposed territory lay between him and the house. He thought of Liz. She was counting on him to rescue her sister. He wanted to do just that for Liz. Somewhere along the way she'd become important to him. Nearly as important as taking down Santini. "Cover me."

"You got it." Nathanial sighted down the barrel of his AK-47.

In military crawl fashion, Blake worked his way down the mound. The icy crust broke, and he sank down into the soft snow beneath as he went, making the going difficult. When he was ten yards away, he rose and ran the short distance to the side of the house and pressed his back against the green siding. He waved a hand at Nathanial, indicating he'd made it unharmed.

Within seconds the NRP officers moved in, their weapons raised at the ready. Drew and Sami joined Blake. He raised a hand and gave the motion to initiate the siege. He sent up another silent prayer that no one would be harmed and they'd be successful. Months of work had gone into finding Santini. Not to mention Liz's distress. This plan had to succeed. He wanted this done and over so they could all go home.

Liz and her sister back to Hilton Head Island, Drew and Sami back to Vancouver, BC, while Blake would return to his studio apartment in Seattle. Though he hadn't intended to stay in the Pacific Northwest city after his first assignment with IBETs, he'd never found a reason to leave either.

And Nathanial…well, Blake wasn't sure where he went between assignments. He knew Nathanial had family on the Big Island Lake Cree reserve in Saskatchewan. But Blake wasn't sure where Nathanial called home.

It occurred to Blake he hadn't done a very good job of befriending his teammate. Even on their last assignment when they'd shared a small cabin on the Idaho Christmas-tree farm where they'd stopped a drug ring from using the farm's tree supply as a means of transporting the illegal substance across the border, their interactions had been about the job at hand, not about their personal lives.

Though now that he thought on it, Nathanial hadn't initiated any deeper conversations either. Guess they both had interpersonal issues.

They approached the front door. Blake nodded to the lead NRP officer who held a small battering ram. The officer lifted the ram and swung. The battering ram hit the door, and the world exploded in a cacophony of noise, flames, heat and smoke.

EIGHT

Liz stared at the cards laid out on the dining table without really seeing the suits or numbers. She couldn't concentrate on the game of solitaire she'd started. Her thoughts were too preoccupied with worry for Jillian and Blake. Blake and his team had left to raid Santini's hideout hours ago and no word had come yet if they'd been successful in taking down Santini and rescuing Jillian.

Giving up on the card game, she rose and went to stand at the picture window overlooking the famed falls.

"It's beautiful, eh?" Teresa Fordham, the female Niagara Regional Police officer, joined her at the window. "I've lived here my whole life, and I never tire of looking at the falls no matter what time of year."

"They're stunning," Liz replied without much enthusiasm. A winter wonderland.

Large ice formations created a spectacular visual feast, but at the moment she couldn't appreciate the view. She should have demanded that Blake let her accompany him and his team. Then she'd at least know what was going on. The not knowing was excruciating.

Teresa's phone rang. She turned away to answer. "Fordham."

The officer let out a small gasp, drawing Liz's attention. The color had drained from the officer's face.

"Casualties?"

Liz sucked in a sharp breath. *Casualties? Oh, no. Please, dear God, no.*

"Yes, sir," Teresa said. "I will, sir."

When she hung up, Liz crossed the room to stand in front of the officer. Panic tightened Liz's chest and constricted her throat. She managed to ask, "What's happened?"

Teresa visibly reined in her emotions and said in a voice devoid of inflection, "There was an explosion."

Clearly she'd been taught to compartmentalize her feelings. A skill Liz didn't possess. Shock took her out at the knees. She staggered and groped for something to hold on to in order to stay upright. Her hand clasped around the top of a dining room chair. She leaned heavily on the wooden prop. "Was my sister…?" Pain lanced through her. "Blake?"

Teresa stepped closer and put a hand on her shoulder. "No one died. Four people were taken to the nearest hospital. I wasn't given names."

"I have to go there," Liz stated in a voice she barely recognized as her own. It was too high-pitched, constricted, panicked.

"I was instructed to keep you here," Teresa said. "For your own safety."

Liz shook her head. She couldn't stay here not knowing if it was her sister or Blake who had been hurt. "What is the name of the hospital?"

"They were taken to Greater Niagara General Hospital."

Fighting tears, Liz asked, "Can you call to find out who was admitted?"

Teresa grimaced with regret. "Sorry. They won't tell me over the phone. Hospital policy."

"Then you have to take me there," Liz pleaded. "I have to know if—" Her voice caught on a sob. *Oh, dear Lord, not Jillian. Not Blake.*

"I can't. I have my orders."

A rush of irritation fueled by fear flamed

through Liz. "I'm not a prisoner here. If you won't take me then I'll go on my own." She headed to the entryway closet for her coat.

Teresa hurried to block the exit. "Please, Liz, I can't let you do that."

Liz shrugged into her coat. "Move out of my way, Officer."

"How are you going to get there?"

The question stopped her. She'd left her purse in her bedroom. She'd need money for a cab or at least the keys to her rental that was parked in the condominium's below-ground parking garage. The car had GPS. She swiveled and ran to her room, snagged her purse from the dresser and then hurried back toward the front door. Teresa remained in place, blocking the door. Frustration pounded at Liz's brain. Her hand flexed around the handle of her purse. "Please move."

Teresa's expression hardened. "No. I was entrusted with your safety."

Short of assaulting the woman, Liz had no options. They were eleven floors up in a high-rise. There was no other exit. She clutched her purse to her chest and clenched her jaw.

The jangle of keys in the lock of the door behind Teresa startled them both. Teresa's hand went to the butt of her gun. Liz's breath stalled.

The door opened, and Blake walked in.

An involuntary cry of relief broke from Liz. She dropped her purse and launched herself at him. He caught her and hugged her close, his arms so strong and secure around her. "You're okay."

"Yes."

Drew, Sami and Nathanial filed into the condo. They looked battle-worn, sporting cuts, bruises and grime.

Jillian wasn't with them.

Liz pushed away from Blake. "Where's my sister?" Horror nose-dived through her. "Oh, no. Please…is she…?"

Teresa had said no one had died. But could Jillian be one of the injured taken to the hospital?

Blake gripped her shoulders and forced her to meet his gaze. She focused on the cuts on his face and the soot smeared on his white snowsuit. Anywhere but his eyes. She didn't want to see her fear confirmed.

"She wasn't there."

It took a moment for his words to sink in. A mix of relief and alarm engulfed her. "What do you mean? I thought you said Santini was there, which meant Jillian was, too? I don't understand? What happened?"

"He had the place rigged to explode," Blake said. "When we breeched the front door it blew up. I was far enough from the blast to react quickly and jumped away from the brunt of the force." He grimaced. "But four Niagara Regional Police officers weren't so fortunate."

"If I'm no longer needed," Teresa interjected. "I'd like to go check on my fellow officers."

Blake nodded at the policewoman, releasing her from her duty of protecting Liz.

"Where is my sister?" Liz repeated, her gaze raking over the four IBETs members.

"Santini must've used that house for years because it had an escape route dug beneath the house that let out a half mile away," Nathanial supplied. "He must've figured we'd trace the call, and gave himself an out, taking your sister with him."

"She's the only leverage he has," Blake added. "He won't hurt her."

"How can you be so sure?" Liz countered. She so wanted to believe him but the longer Santini held her sister captive, the harder it was for Liz to believe the madman would ever let Jillian go alive.

Blake stared at her, seemingly at a loss for

words. He couldn't be sure. Not really. He could speculate, assume and even pray that Santini wouldn't harm Jillian, but no one could have predicted Santini would blow up his hideout. So it stood to reason no one could foresee what Santini would do now. Liz knew their only course of action was to follow through on Santini's demand that she bring the necklace to Queen Victoria Park at the appointed time.

Fine. Whatever it took. She was not going to fail Jillian.

"Looks like I'm going to the park tonight," Liz said as she stripped off her coat. She laid it over a chair. "I suggest we come up with a strategy because time is ticking away."

Blake muted his mic so that Liz couldn't hear him through the earpiece placed in her right ear. "I hate this whole scenario," he said to Nathanial.

They waited in a van outside of Queen Victoria Park monitoring Liz's movements as she made her way through the throng of people who'd come out tonight to enjoy the annual Winter Festival of Lights despite the winter chill. She was wired with a mic, an ear link and a small button camera. The uncut diamond necklace was inside the box that was tucked inside her coat.

Now that the snowstorm had abated, the thick layer of white created a beautiful backdrop reflecting the multitude of displays ranging from 3-D illuminated Canadian wildlife, the world's largest illuminated Canadian/American flag and the iconic shimmering Zimmerman Fountain.

On the video feed from Liz's button camera he caught glimpses of food vendors and tents for kids' activities. The happy sound of the festivalgoers was muffled by the roar of the falls. Even though the top layers of the river were frozen, the water beneath still churned at a near deafening decibel.

"You need to chill," Nathanial said. "She's doing great. Drew and Sami have eyes on her. Nothing's going to go wrong."

"After what happened today? How can you say that?" They'd never even considered Santini would have an underground escape route, though they should have, considering Santini was as close to a rat as they'd ever pursued. Blake should have anticipated Santini having a getaway tunnel. Blake should have anticipated the explosion. And that he'd been caught unaware annoyed and frustrated him to no end. Guilt at the thought of the wounded men gnawed at his conscience. Their injuries were on his head. Anger simmered below the surface. Anger at himself, anger at Santini. Anger at God for allowing good men to be hurt by a criminal like Idris Santini.

Nathanial arched one black eyebrow. "Santini may be slippery and crafty, but he's just a man. Not some superpowered villain. We have officers in place all over the park. There's no way Santini will slip through our grasp again."

Blake wasn't taking any chances. They'd placed a tracker on the necklace in case Santini managed to circumvent their surveillance before they could apprehend him. That way Blake and the team could concentrate on protecting Liz and reclaiming her sister. That was if Santini followed through and brought Jillian to the park for the exchange. Blake had his doubts Santini would show. Last time he'd sent Travis to do his dirty work. Would Santini send another of his henchmen? And what of this Ken fellow? Was he stalking Liz or still after the necklace?

Blake studied the monitors showing the camera feed from Liz's button camera as well as four other video feeds they'd positioned in optimal places throughout the park. He looked for a man in a fedora. But he knew that Ken probably would have ditched the hat, so Blake studied the faces of every man, hunting for Santini and Ken.

The sound of a phone ringing brought Blake's senses into pinpoint focus. He shifted into high alert. It was Liz's cell phone. They heard her answer but they couldn't hear the other end of the conversation.

"Where?" Liz's voice rose. "Okay. I'm heading there now."

She hung up. "That was Santini."

Blake flipped on the ear link. "What are your instructions?"

He—" her voice cut out. The roar of the falls overwhelmed the mic.

"Liz!" Adrenaline zipped through his veins. "Liz, can you hear me?"

Nothing.

The link wasn't picking up her voice and he had a sinking feeling she couldn't hear him over the rush of the water. Her button camera showed him she'd moved closer to the falls. He relayed that to Drew.

"Copy. We'll head that way."

Blake swiftly rose and grabbed his coat.

"Where are you going?" Nathanial asked.

"Santini will spot you and then this whole sting will be a bust."

"I can't leave her out there without being able to communicate with her," Blake said. He'd made a promise to protect her.

"She's not unguarded. You heard Drew. He and Sami are on her trail."

"I need to be out there," Blake insisted. If anything happened to her…he didn't think he could take any more guilt. A mocking voice inside his head scoffed because the real reason he dreaded anything happening to Liz was that he cared for her. There. He'd admitted it. He cared. He wasn't totally unfeeling. She was a smart, gutsy and beautiful woman who inspired admiration and respect. What wasn't there to care about, to like?

"Dude, you have issues with control."

Blake glowered at his friend. "I don't need you to psychoanalyze me."

Besides, needing to control what happened to Liz had more to do with Blake's growing feelings for her than his control-freak tendencies. Boy, would Nathanial love to analyze that.

Nathanial held up his hand in entreaty. "Hey, I'm just telling it like it is. You have to trust the rest of us to get the job done."

Knowing his friend and colleague was right, Blake ran a hand through his hair and plopped back down in the chair, his gaze riveted to the video feeds. Liz had gone out of view of the other cameras. He had only her button camera to monitor her whereabouts. She was near the platform of the tunnel running beneath the falls. He frowned, not liking how close she stood to the railing that prevented visitors from plunging over the side into the churning water below.

"Drew?" Blake tried reaching the Canadian but his communication link wasn't responding either. "This is weird. I think their comms are being blocked."

"I agree," Nathanial said. He typed into the computer to his left. "I'm hacking into the city's camera network to see if I can get a clearer, wider view of the platform.

No go. All the angles were too far left or right. There didn't appear to be any cameras centered on the platform or the entrance to the tunnels. "I have a bad feeling about this." Blake's hands grew damp with anxiety. "Knowing Santini I'm sure he's set up some sort of trap, and she's going to walk right into it like an insect drawn to a spider's web."

* * *

Liz tapped her ear, barely holding off the panic rising up inside. "Blake? Blake, can you hear me?"

Between the laughter and voices of the many visitors to the park and the constant roar of the falls, she could hardly hear herself talk. She glanced around, searching for one of the officers or Drew and Sami. She knew they were near, keeping a close eye on her. The knowledge gave her a measure of comfort but didn't ease the tension in her shoulders.

She also knew Blake could see where she was via the small camera disguised as a button attached to her coat. Sami had done the honors of replacing her black coat button with the camera. No one would notice the difference in buttons unless they looked closely. Even then it wouldn't be unreasonable to assume she'd lost a button and replaced it with another that didn't match the others.

At least that was what she hoped Santini would think if she came face-to-face with him.

She replayed Santini's instructions through her mind. He'd said to go to the entrance of the tunnels that ran beneath the falls. She reached the platform without trouble. The ice spray from the falls stung her skin and dampened her uncovered hair. Her coat thankfully had a water-resistant protective shell. Tourists crowded around the ice-crusted railing taking pictures of the frozen layer of water or taking selfies with the falls in the background. She glanced over the edge. The dizzying height had her stepping quickly back.

She spied the tunnel entrance. She shuddered and broke out in a cold sweat. Good thing she didn't have to go inside there. A long sign bearing the Canadian flag dripped with icicles. The stairs leading to the heavy metal door were roped off with caution tape. No doubt the steps where iced over as well and much too dangerous for anyone to negotiate.

She searched for the little dark-haired woman who'd pressed the first note into her hand at Fort George. They hadn't been able to find her after she'd hurried off. So Liz half expected her to show up again. No one matching what Liz remembered of the woman was anywhere nearby. Her attention went back to the door. It was ajar. She moved closer, unsure what to expect. Another note? Should she enter? The thought made her go numb.

Her sister could be on the other side of that door.

Or it could be a trap. Most likely was a trap.

She turned away from the entrance to survey the area once again. No one seemed to be paying her any heed. Yet, she had the distinct sensation of being watched. It was just Drew and Sami, she chided herself.

She refocused her attention on the tunnel. Her breath hitched. Did she dare check the tunnel in case her sister was inside? Santini had said to go to the entrance of the tunnels. Had he meant enter the tunnels? She clasped her hands together to still the tremor running rampant through her limbs.

Dear Lord, I need you now more than ever. Give me the strength, the courage.

She was so scared. But she had to be brave. For her sister. For herself. For Blake. She wanted him to be proud of her and to know that she wasn't a wimp who crumbled when things became hard. She could do this.

Before she could change her mind, she ducked beneath the caution tape, grasped the railing handle and carefully made her way up the steps to the door. Using both hands, she pulled the door open enough to slip inside.

The tunnel wasn't nearly as small as she'd envisioned which provided a bubble of relief.

A dimly lit elevator waited. The doors opened, and a bare bulb provided a guiding light. She inwardly groaned. She hated elevators. The thought of being trapped inside the tiny space made her break out in hives.

But her sister's life was on the line. She would do anything to save Jillian, including braving her fear of enclosed spaces. Seeing no other option but to enter the car, she did and tried not to think about the four walls, the low ceiling and the isolation. The panic of being trapped lurked at the edges of her mind.

There was only a down button. She pushed it. The doors slid closed. Her lungs seized, and her body tensed as the elevator descended. She counted the seconds. One-one thousand. Two-one thousand. Three-one thousand. Four-one thousand. Five…

When the doors opened, she took a deep breath, filling her lungs with musty air, and rushed out of the elevator. The bare bulb from inside the elevator car provided a small circle of light. The tunnel ceiling was so low she could reach up and touch the cold surface. This tunnel wasn't like the one above. Here she could feel the walls closing in, feel the way her skin crawled with the need to escape, but she remained rooted to the tunnel floor. The elevator doors closed behind her, leaving her in complete blackness. Cold fingers of panic clawed up her throat. She forced herself to breathe.

She stared into the darkness, fighting the burning need to turn around and retreat. Then a light flared farther down the long corridor. A beacon she prayed would take her to her sister. A terrorized storm of anxiety hit her full force and shifted into the shadows.

Had she been right that this was a trap? If she moved toward the light what would she find? Would she be walking toward her death?

Needing a moment to calm her racing heart, she leaned against the rough wall. The wet cold of the wall seeped through her coat. Taking deep breaths, she removed her mother's jewelry box, holding the necklace, from inside her jacket and opened the case to slip the necklace from the velvet bed.

For a moment she held the stones in a fierce grip. Even through her gloves they felt cold and alien. These jewels had caused so many traumas. She sent up a plea to God that she could rid herself of this burden and get her sister back safely. Her hands shook as she stuffed the stones back into the box and then the box back inside her jacket.

Bolstering her courage and forcing back the anxiety twisting through her, she stepped into the darkness and moved toward the light.

NINE

Liz's video feed plunged into darkness, and Blake's heart took a plunge, too. Not even the light displays of the festival could be seen. She'd gone into the tunnel beneath the falls. Alone.

During normal operating hours the tunnel would be teeming with people. The tunnel had been built as a tourist attraction and was reachable by an elevator. At this hour it was now cordoned off because of the ice that had accumulated on the stairs. That the door had been pried open meant that Santini must now be inside. And so was Liz.

Blake couldn't sit by any longer. He had to go to her. He had to make sure she was safe, protected. Not because he didn't trust his team or the Niagara Regional Police officers, but...well, he couldn't articulate the exact reason at the moment, not with all of his instincts screaming go, go!

He jumped up, grabbed his jacket and took off out of the van as if his feet were on fire. He was vaguely aware that Nathanial was right on his heels.

"Liz is in the tunnel," Blake shouted into his communication link, praying the others would hear. "Head to the tunnels."

He and Nathanial pushed their way through the crowds to the tunnel entrance that would lead them behind the falls. Drew and Sami joined them.

Blake ripped aside the caution tape and stepped onto the first step. The bottoms of his snow boots skidded on the slick ice covering the stairs, but he managed to reach the landing in one piece.

"Careful," he murmured to the others behind him.

A small button in the wall glowed a dull yellow. He pushed it, and the elevator doors slid open. He, Nathanial, Drew and Sami crowded into the car. He pressed the button that would take them to the tunnel level.

Before the elevator door opened, Nathanial unscrewed the car's lone light bulb. Darkness surrounded them, and Blake belatedly wished he'd thought to grab a set of night vision goggles from the van. He had a flashlight attached to his belt but decided to use the advantage of surprise the darkness offered.

He was alarmed Santini hadn't led Liz to one of the festival attractions and done the exchange in a public setting where there was more likelihood of potential hostages or collateral damage.

What purpose did Santini have for luring Liz into the bowels of the tunnel with only one way in or out? Unless he'd somehow gained admittance through the maintenance access points. Did he intend to kidnap Liz in addition to her sister? Or was his plan to grab the necklace and kill both women, leaving their corpses in the tunnels to be found when the ice thawed?

Blake's stomach plummeted at the dire scenario. He sent up a silent plea to God above that he wasn't too late, that he wouldn't fail Liz.

How could he live with himself if he did?

The cold of the dank underground tunnel beneath Niagara Falls seeping through Liz's jacket, sweater and long-sleeved T-shirt chilled her skin. She stifled the urge to jog to

keep warm. She hated being in such a confined space. She had to force her mind not to
consider the dim surroundings.

Instead, she moved with caution toward the
glowing light she'd spotted after exiting the
elevator. She half expected Santini, or some
other thug, to jump out at her like in some
creepy carnival fun house. Shadows created
by the glow danced on the wall, providing
an eerie display that had the fine hairs at the
base of her neck rising.

There was nothing fun about this, in fact,
she was scared silly. Every step was torture.
Her chest hurt with the force of each heartbeat. But for Jillian's sake, Liz would face
down her terror and continue to fight for her
safety.

However, she'd give anything to have Blake
at her side. Strange how quickly she'd learned
to rely on him. To trust him. He could be
closed off at times, yet she sensed a deep well
of emotion lay within him that he refused to
tap into. She was sure his ability to contain
his feelings helped make him an excellent
agent.

And she needed him to be a superagent
now. She prayed he'd have her back.

She found the light source in an alcove

beneath a frosted window, which during the summer would give a spectacular view of the churning falls. A small battery-operated dome light sat on the concrete floor, creating an illuminated circle.

The hairs on her arms rose in alarm. There was movement behind her. She whipped around to find three men and her sister emerging from the shadows.

One of the men held a gun aimed at her, but her attention was riveted to her sister. Thick black tape covered Jillian's mouth, and her hands were tied together in front of her. Her big blue eyes brimmed with tears of terror.

Relief at seeing Jillian alive was tempered by the fact that one of the thugs had his beefy hand clasped around Jillian's biceps. The dim lighting couldn't conceal the fear in Jillian's eyes nor her disheveled appearance. At least she had on the thick winter coat Liz had insisted she buy for her honeymoon to Niagara.

The shorter of the three men stepped forward. He was stocky, with light brown hair swept back from a round face. He had a pugilist's nose and heavy jowls. Muddied brown eyes studied her with a calculated gleam.

He sneered at her, lifting one corner of his thick lips. He wore a long wool coat that nearly touched the tips of his expensive-looking snow boots. His hands were buried in his coat pockets.

This could only be Santini, Liz thought. No one could ooze as much arrogance as a man who thought he was beyond the law. But she needed to make sure. "Santini?"

"Yes. And you're the sister?" Santini said. "Not much resemblance."

He was right. Jillian was the exact opposite of Liz.

But none of that mattered.

Liz swallowed hard and lifted her chin and tried not to let him undermine her confidence even as she shied away from the consequences of not succeeding. Somehow, someway, Liz would honor her promise to their father and save Jillian.

Refusing to give Santini the satisfaction of rising to his baited statement, she ignored him and yanked the box from her coat pocket. "You wanted this."

"That I do." He held out his hand. "Give me the necklace."

"Release my sister," Liz said with as much bravado as she could muster.

She had no idea how she and Jillian were going to get out of this situation alive. Liz

prayed that Blake and his team were closing in. They had to have seen her enter the
tunnel through the button camera now facing Santini.

Santini stroked his chin with blunt fingers.
His chuckle echoed off the walls. "You do realize I can't allow you to leave, don't you?"

She swallowed back panic. She didn't want
to die, not yet, not before she'd had a chance
to tell Blake she…she what? She shook her
head, shoving aside thoughts of Blake, and
fought her fear. She needed to strategize. The
only exit she was aware of was behind her
through the dark.

But first Santini had to release her sister.
"You can have the necklace. Just let my sister go."

Santini gestured to his henchmen. "Let the
sisters reunite."

The thug shoved Jillian at Liz. Jillian stumbled. Liz caught her before she could fall to
her knees. Turning her away from Santini,
Liz wrapped her arms around Jillian and
whispered, "Get ready to run."

Jillian whimpered and vigorously shook
her head.

Liz stepped back to gauge Jillian's strange
reaction. What was wrong with her?

Keeping her arm around her sister, Liz faced Santini and extended the box toward him. He snatched it from her hand and removed the necklace. He threw her mother's box to the side like a piece of trash.

She gritted her teeth and fought the urge to snag it from the ground. The important issue was for her and Jillian to escape. She knew the tracker on the necklace would lead Blake and his team to Santini when he left the tunnel.

Keeping his attention on examining the diamonds, Santini said to his thugs, "Kill them."

Liz's heart pitched, and panicked adrenaline pumped in her veins. She had to act. Now.

Liz propelled Jillian toward the darkness just as Blake and Nathanial stepped out of the inky shadows to move in on Santini and his thugs. Drew and Sami also emerged from the black tunnel and stayed slightly behind Blake and Nathanial since the tunnel wasn't wide enough for them to stand shoulder to shoulder.

Overwhelming relief made Liz's knees weak. She'd prayed Blake would arrive in time. God had answered her prayer, showing her Blake was a man she could count on. Now they were saved. Blake would take down Santini.

And this nightmare would finally come to an end.

"Federal agents. Drop your weapons," Blake ordered as he positioned himself in front of Liz, using himself as a shield to protect her and Jillian. Drew, Sami and Nathanial flanked Blake.

The show of force obviously intimidated the thugs with the guns. The two men slowly lowered their weapons to the ground.

The tightness in Blake's chest eased at the sight of Liz unharmed. He'd arrived in time, with seconds to spare. Undoubtedly Santini would have ordered his thugs to shoot the two women the moment he had what he wanted. The thought grabbed Blake by the throat. He needed to get the women out of there. They still weren't completely safe.

Liz struggled to untie the thin piece of rope keeping Jillian's hands together. Jillian whimpered again. "I know, honey," Liz said. "Let me get you untied and you can take the tape off your mouth."

"Show me your hand," Nathanial shouted

at Santini who still had one hand shoved into his coat pocket while his other hand held the necklace.

The man's mouth stretched into an evil smile. A shudder of distaste washed over Blake. This was the first face-to-face encounter with the criminal he'd been chasing to avenge his partner's death, and Blake couldn't wait to slap cuffs on the man. "You heard him. Take your hand out of your pocket."

"With pleasure." Santini withdrew his hand from his coat pocket holding a small device.

Blake's gut clenched. A detonator. Was it a dead man's switch? A suicide vest? He hadn't pegged Santini as the type who would rather die than go to jail.

"Did you think I'd come unprepared?" Santini taunted. "You federal boys keep underestimating me."

Anger ticked through Blake, but he kept his focus on the detonator in Santini's hand. "We know exactly what you are. A criminal. A killer."

Santini shrugged. "I do what I have to. Not my fault when one of you feds—" he squinted at Nathanial and Drew "—or Canucks, get in my way and end up on a slab in the morgue."

"Lizzie, listen to me," Jillian said once Liz had the tape off her mouth.

"Lizzie," Santini mimicked. "I'm so sick of hearing about Lizzie. *Lizzie will save me. Lizzie won't let you hurt me.* I've half a mind to blow you to bits just because. But I want to leave with my diamonds, and if you don't let me…*boom*." His beady eyes twinkled with maniacal amusement.

"What are you talking about?" Nathanial asked, as he edged closer.

"Go on, Jillian, show them," Santini said.

Fat tears rolled down Jillian's cheeks. She carefully unbuttoned her coat to reveal an improvised explosive belt wrapped around her waist.

Liz's gasp ricocheted off the walls.

Jillian sniffled.

Liz put her arm around her sister and cooed soft soothing words. "It'll be okay. You'll see."

He couldn't fail Liz. Not when they were so close to gaining justice for his friend Liam and freeing Jillian. Not when his feelings about Liz were a hot, confused knot in his heart. His hand tightened on the grip of his gun, his finger hovering over the trigger.

"You'd blow yourself and your men up, too," Drew pointed out. "You know that, right?"

Santini's expression showed nothing, no regret or sympathy for his two thugs who stared at their boss with horror.

Blake calculated the distance between Nathanial and Santini. How quickly could Nathanial dive for the detonator if Blake put a bullet in Santini?

Blake glanced at Nathanial. He shook his head, indicating he didn't see an option. They were too far away from Santini. Frustration fueled Blake's brain to work the angles and find a solution. He stepped closer to Liz.

The only bargaining chip they had was in Santini's hand. Blake lifted the barrel of his gun so it was no longer trained on Santini. "Just set the detonator on the ground and walk away," Blake said. "You have what you wanted."

He was confident that the Niagara Regional Police would apprehend Santini the second he stepped outside. And if he managed to slip past them, the tracker on the necklace would allow them to follow him and capture him.

Santini arched an eyebrow. His brown eyes blazed with mockery. "How about we all walk out of here nice and easy, then I'll relinquish the detonator."

Really? Santini was crafty and wily. There

was no way he couldn't suspect there were more officers on the other side of the tunnel door. He had something up his sleeve, but Blake's priority was to get everyone out of the tunnel alive. He'd have to trust the others to swoop in and disarm Santini before he had an opportunity to press the button and blow them all to smithereens.

"Okay, we all walk out of here," Blake said. "Keep your hands in the air where we can see them."

At the elevator, Nathanial screwed the bulb back in before they crammed inside. Blake put an arm around Liz, drawing her up against his chest. He ignored the curious glances from the others. He couldn't explain even if he wanted to. All he knew was he needed to feel her close. It was so weird to be in the tight confines of the elevator with the man he'd been hunting for months and knowing that with one wrong twitch, Santini could blow them all to bits.

When they reached the entry point, they filed out. Drew, Sami and the Cantrell sisters brought up the rear.

"I was afraid I'd die down there," Jillian said with a visible shiver.

They weren't out of the woods yet. They

still needed to get the detonator and disarm the explosive device strapped to Jillian's middle.

Once they were outside, Santini said, "You tell your people to back off." He gestured to the dozen officers now pointing their weapons at him. "Unless you want me to blow us all to kingdom come? You do realize the explosion will cause catastrophic damage to the falls and the city."

Blake motioned for everyone to lower their weapons. "Satisfied?" He stepped toward him. "Now hand it over."

"Send Liz over. She and I will walk away and then I'll hand her the detonator."

"No way," Blake said. "You give it to me."

"No. I want to give it to *Lizzie*." Santini gestured to Liz.

"Not happening," Blake repeated and took another step forward. "Come on, Santini, work with me here."

"Don't come any closer." Santini's thumb grazed over the detonator's red button.

Blake clenched his jaw. He seriously wanted to do the man bodily harm.

Liz touched Blake's arm, diverting his concentration. "I'll do it," she said, her voice whisper soft.

He captured her hand. A fierce protectiveness swept through him. "No. I won't allow it."

"Blake, it's a small price to pay for everyone else's safety."

An odd burn of emotion gripped his chest and clogged his throat. He forced out the words, "I don't trust him."

Her blue-green gaze softened and she squeezed his arm. "But I trust you." Her voice dropped even lower, so that only he could hear. "You'll find me."

Her words speared clean through him to the core of his being. Not so many days ago he'd told her she had no choice but to trust him. But that hadn't been true.

He'd wanted her to trust him because he needed her to, but she did have a choice. And now she freely gave her trust to him.

She believed in him. He'd never felt so humbled.

Everything inside of him raged against letting her sacrifice herself. But the ICE agent in him knew he had to let her go. They'd put a tracking device on the necklace. They would follow and wait until she was safe before swooping in and arresting Santini.

"Lizzie, no," Jillian pleaded. "He's evil."

Without breaking her hold on Blake's arm, Liz turned to her sister. "I love you, Jillian. But I have to do this."

Jillian wept. Blake sympathized with her. He wanted to weep, to howl, to ram his fist into Santini's smug face. The muscles in Blake's neck and shoulders stiffened to an unbearable pain that matched the searing burn in his heart.

When Liz refocused her attention on Blake, he saw the love in her eyes directed at him. His mouth turned to cotton. Seeing that tender look scared him nearly as much as letting her go with a madman.

Liz squared her shoulders and released his arm. As she walked toward Santini, it took every ounce of self-control Blake had not to grab her and haul her back to his side.

Santini's grin turned Blake's stomach.

When Liz reached Santini, he snatched her hand and yanked her to him. Blake lunged forward. Nathanial held him back as Santini wrapped one thick arm around her throat while still holding the explosive trigger in his hand.

"Everyone move back," Santini yelled. "Let us pass, and then I'll release your friend."

Fury erupted in Blake's chest and mushroomed into a dark cloud over his head. His hands curled into fists at his sides. As he watched Santini drag Liz away, Blake threw up a prayer and plea for God to keep her safe.

The arm snaked around Liz's shoulders pressed hard on her throat, cutting off her air supply. She clawed at his arm to no avail. He smelled of menthol, a scent she associated with death. The hospice care nurse had used a menthol cream on her mother to help soothe the pain of the cancer that had ravished her body. Liz's stomach heaved, and she gagged, which only made breathing more difficult.

To keep her panic at bay, she kept her eyes trained on Blake, who followed them at a distance as Santini dragged her away. She memorized each line in his handsome face, each angle and plane of his cheeks and jaw.

Blake's voice sounded in her head. "It's going to be okay. I won't lose you."

Her heart ached with fear and longing. She'd wanted so badly to tell Blake that somewhere along the way she'd fallen in love with him. Even though she knew doing so wasn't smart.

There was no future for them.

She belonged on Hilton Head Island, belonged at the store that her father had started and left to her and Jillian. And now that Jillian's husband was in jail, she would need Liz to help her pick up the pieces of her broken heart.

Whereas Blake would move on to his next mission, as he should. He protected both the United States and Canada in ways she'd never imagined from threats large and small. He was a hero.

And she knew deep inside if she let herself, she could easily lose herself in him and become just like her father with no identity outside of the person she loved.

One half of a whole that couldn't survive alone.

That was something she couldn't allow, despite how proud and in awe she was of Blake. She knew how hard it had been for him to let her go. He'd wanted to retain control of the situation, but life didn't always allow that. Only God was in control.

With both Blake and God on her side, she would survive this ordeal. But that knowledge didn't keep the fear from clawing through her.

Santini hauled her toward a dark SUV waiting at the curb just outside the festival boundary. His thugs hustled in front of him.

Taking shallow breaths, Liz kept her gaze locked on Blake, who remained far enough away to not spook Santini into following through with his threat.

Santini popped open the driver's-side door and commanded, "Get in!"

Terror lanced through her. She struggled against his surprisingly strong arm. "You said you'd give me the detonator and release me."

"Get in," Santini repeated. "Or I blow your sister and everyone else into bits."

Where would he take her? What would he do with her? She calmed herself with the knowledge that Blake would be able to hear her through the wire in her coat pocket and see through the camera attached to her button.

But what about the explosives attached to her sister? Liz searched for Jillian, but she couldn't see her among the crowd gathering to watch the spectacle of Santini forcing Liz into his SUV.

From the crazy gleam in Santini's eyes, she knew with a deep gut certainty he wasn't bluffing. She scrambled into the driver's seat of the vehicle.

"Keep going," he said, shoving at her as he crawled inside behind her.

Clambering over the middle console, she landed in the passenger seat in a heap. Behind her, one of the thugs snickered at her ungainly entrance. As she righted herself and shot the big lug a vehement glare, Santini locked the doors and then started the engine. Still holding on to the detonator with one hand, he pressed on the gas and the SUV shot forward. He cranked the wheel, barely avoiding pedestrians who'd stopped to gawk.

"Where are you taking me?" Liz grappled with the seat belt and buckled herself in.

"Shut up!" He sped through stoplights, swerving around cars, drifting into the oncoming traffic lane. Horns blared. Liz braced herself, sure that any second they'd be struck. But they managed to leave the city limits unscathed.

"Liz, I'm here," Blake's voice entered her head. "We're following you. We have an explosives specialist working on the bomb strapped to Jillian."

She nearly wept with relief. But she knew she couldn't rejoice yet. The specialist could miscalculate, or Santini could have rigged the explosives with a secondary trigger that could explode if tampered with.

"Please, give me the detonator," she implored.

Without answering, he rolled the window down and chucked the detonator out.

Liz's mouth dropped open. "You threw the detonator out the window," she said for Blake's benefit. That was unexpected. But she wouldn't complain.

He cackled. "Are you sure that was the detonator?"

Her fingers curled into fists. He was toying with her, enjoying her suffering. "You have what you want. You said you'd let me go."

"No way, sweetheart, you're my insurance policy." He exited the main highway onto a side street without any streetlights. He brought the vehicle to an abrupt halt on the shoulder.

Not sure what to think, anxiety snaked through Liz. She grabbed the handle to open the door, but it was locked. She tried the lock mechanism. It didn't work. He must have it on parental control. "Why have you stopped?"

He snorted "Do you think I'm stupid? Do you think I don't know the way the law operates? I haven't been able to evade capture this long without anticipating my opponents' moves."

He reached across her to open the glove box. He grabbed a pistol and what looked to Liz like a walkie-talkie. He slammed the glove compartment closed. Then he fiddled with controls on the walkie-talkie.

Red lights glowed from the device, filling in the shadows and distorting Santini's face. Liz shrank back as he lifted the thing and waved it over her. It let out long, shrill beeps.

Santini's lips thinned. "I knew you were bugged."

Her stomach sank. So the device wasn't a walkie-talkie but an electronic detector. "It's okay, Liz. Keep calm," Blake said into her ear. "We're not that far behind you."

"Take off your coat," Santini demanded, drawing her attention.

She shrugged out of the jacket. He grabbed it, rolled down the window and threw it out. Then he waved the handheld detector over her again. It remained silent until he brought it near her ear. The shrill alarm reverberated through Liz's head. Santini grabbed her by the hair and yanked her close. His thick fingers plucked at her ear.

She swatted his hand away and fished the small communication link from her ear and held it out to him. "There. Are you satisfied? Now will you let me go?"

He tossed the earpiece out the window, then without comment, restarted the engine and continued driving deeper into the woods.

Liz said a silent prayer of thanksgiving that Santini hadn't thought to swipe his device over the necklace. The tracker attached to the backside of one of the stones was now her only hope of rescue.

TEN

Liz hid her surprise when Santini turned the SUV down a snow-rutted road leading to an airport. Huge lights illuminated the runway and glistened off the snow piled high on the edges of the long runway.

A large gate blocked their path. Santini slowed to a stop and rolled down the window. He removed his wallet from the inside pocket of his coat and slipped an electronic key card out and swiped it against the box right outside the driver's-side door. The gate opened.

Obviously he'd been here before and apparently planned on executing his escape via airplane. She noticed a dark helicopter off to the side. Maybe not a plane. A shiver of apprehension tripped over her skin. She'd never been in a helicopter and certainly didn't want to experience it now.

He brought the vehicle to a halt outside of

a huge blue metal building on the far side of a short, squat air traffic control tower. Tall red-tipped antennas grew out of the top of the tower. Dark-tinted windows concealed the control personnel inside. But would they be able to see her? There had to be a way to signal to them that she was in distress.

Killing the engine, Santini turned to her with the gun aimed at her heart. "No funny business, you hear me? We're going to get out nice and easy, then we're going to make our way inside the hangar. I've got a plane waiting."

Wariness threaded through her. "I'm not going with you."

He shoved the gun closer to her face. "Yes, you are. Now move."

She swallowed back the tide of terror rising up to scorch her throat. She'd switched places with Jillian. Would she end up with an explosive wrapped around her? Or would Santini just shoot her? Deciding it was better to comply than argue with him, she opened the door and stepped out.

The frigid air seeped through her clothes to chill her all the way to her marrow. She'd never liked winter but now she positively detested it. She contemplated running for the tower, but feared he'd blast a hole in her back if she tried. She had to be patient and wait for an opportunity. She prayed God would orchestrate a moment when she could escape unharmed.

Santini rounded the front end of the SUV, snagged her arm and forced her to walk toward the large rectangular building. His two thugs climbed out and trudged along behind them like lap dogs. High square windows marched across the building and glowed from within.

She glanced over her shoulder, past the two thugs, hoping to see the cavalry, in the form of Blake and his team, coming to her rescue. The last thing she'd heard Blake say was that they weren't far behind. But would they make it in time before Santini escaped? And what about her? Would Santini really take her with him? Or would he kill her inside the airplane hangar?

Dread churned in her tummy. With each step, uncertainty of what was to come ratcheted her unease to a near blinding terror. One thug hustled to open the large metal door. The grating sound amplified her fear. She cringed.

Santini pulled her inside the large hangar. Several more men waited inside with a uniformed pilot holding a clipboard in his hand. Large skylights let in the moon's glow to bathe a sleek dual-engine private jet. The plane's door was open with stairs spilling out.

A stranglehold of alarm urged Liz to do what she could to keep from boarding that plane. Because once she did, she had a feeling her usefulness would evaporate and Santini would dispose of her. She needed to put up a struggle, to buy Blake time to arrive.

A shadow passed overhead, distracting Santini. He glanced up, affording her the moment she'd been praying for. She dug in her heels and with a quick twist broke free of Santini's grip.

"Hey!" he shouted. "Where do you think you're going?"

She ran for the big hangar door, hoping to escape, hoping not everyone on the ground crew was a thug of Santini's. She prayed that one of them would run interference.

"Get her!" Santini bellowed, dispelling her hope that the men weren't all criminals.

She let loose a loud scream. Maybe she could at least draw attention from the tower. Surely, they'd send airport security if they heard a scream and saw a woman running for her life.

The sound of pounding feet on the hangar's concrete floor spurred her to sprint faster. She passed through the open hangar door. A large hand clamped on her arm and yanked sideways. Panicked, she lashed out, her fists glancing off wide shoulders.

"Liz!" Blake's voice registered in her frantic mind.

She stilled. Sure she was imagining him, she blinked several times. "Blake?"

He wrapped one arm about her waist and spun her around so that she was behind him. In his other arm he carried a large rifle with a scope aimed at the men who'd chased after her. Sami, Drew and Nathanial joined them. The men halted. A little red dot appeared on each man's chest. The odds that the men and woman trained in firearms wouldn't hit their target was low. Enough so that Santini's men dropped their weapons and lifted their hands. Smart on their part.

From inside the hangar the sound of the skylights shattering filled the air. Blake stalked forward. Liz grabbed a handful of his jacket and moved in tandem with him. They entered the hangar. A dozen officers dressed in black tactical gear bearing large weapons had rappelled through the opening.

They landed on the ground surrounding Santini and his men.

"Put down your weapons," Blake demanded.

Santini dropped his gun and sneered at Blake. "You. I should have killed you when I killed that other agent. I saw you on the pier. I knew you'd be trouble. Ever since then you've been a thorn in my side."

Liz could see the tension in Blake's shoulders, could feel his rage. She held her breath. Why would Santini bait Blake?

"A mistake you'll have to live with." Blake reached behind him to gently remove her hand from his coat, forcing her to let him go. Then in two long strides he was standing nose to nose with Santini. "You're done."

A sly smile spread Santini's lips. "We'll see."

Blake placed a hand on Santini's shoulder and forced him to his knees. "Hands behind your back."

Santini complied, but the almost bored expression on his face made Liz's blood boil. The man was so smug. So sure that he was above the law. But he wasn't.

Blake had succeeded in bringing Santini to justice.

Pride and awe filled her. Blake was a man

of his word. A man worthy of her trust and her love.

She caught her breath. She did love him, but she had no idea what to do about it. If she confessed to him how she felt, what good would that do? She needed to hold on tight to her emotions. Keep them within her heart because there wasn't room in his life for her and she couldn't give up her identity for love.

Blake reached into Santini's coat pockets until he found the necklace. "You won't need this where you're going."

Blake gestured for the officers to take Santini into custody. Then he returned to her. After slipping the uncut-diamond strand into his pocket, he smoothed back a lock of her hair. The rough pads of his fingers were gentle against her skin. The words *I love you* hovered on her tongue.

But she couldn't bring herself to utter them. She wasn't that brave.

"I'll take you to your sister," Blake said.

Blinking back the burn of tears, she nodded. "Where is she?"

"At the hospital."

Her stomach dropped. "She's hurt?"

One corner of his mouth lifted. "No. Minor

scrapes and bruises. But she sure put up one whopper of a fit."

Liz smiled, glad to know her sister's spirit hadn't been broken. "She's a bit of a drama queen."

Blake chuckled. "So Drew tells me. He and Sami are with her."

Slinging his rifle over his shoulder, he grasped her hand and tucked it within the crook of his arm. "Come on."

She glanced back at Santini being led to a waiting vehicle. "Don't you want to take him in?"

He kept his gaze on her. "Nathanial and the others can handle the transport."

Sighing, she leaned into him. Her chest crowded with love for this very special agent. "I'm glad this ordeal is over."

He helped her into a black SUV. They were the first of the vehicles to leave the airport. The rest stayed behind to process the scene and handle those arrested. He cranked the heater, and Liz tilted her head back onto the headrest. The beams of the SUV's front lights cut through the darkness. A truck sat parked on the side of the road.

"That's strange," Blake remarked as they

passed the truck. "There was no truck there on our way in."

She looked through the back window in time to see two dark figures jump into the truck, then the vehicle lights came on. Alarmed, she sat up. "Uh, Blake?"

The truck whipped a U-turn and raced toward them.

"I see them." Blake pressed the gas pedal. They shot forward, the rear tires fishtailing in the snow. The pickup truck sped closer. The truck crossed into the oncoming traffic lane and tried to pull even with their SUV. The back passenger window behind Blake exploded in a shower of glass.

"Get down!" Blake shouted. He swerved to block the truck, throwing Liz sideways. She grasped the door handle and scrunched down as best she could given the seat belt had locked in place and was cutting into her.

The truck hit the SUV's back bumper. The vehicle's rear tires slid sideways, but Blake managed to keep from losing control. Liz closed her eyes and sent up a fervent plea to God for protection.

She'd thought the nightmare was over, but no. "It's Ken, isn't it?" It had to be Ken and his cohort. Who else could it be? But how had they have found them?

"Hang on." Sharp determination laced his words.

He hit the brakes hard and swerved, forcing the truck to shoot past them to keep from a full collision. Then Blake stepped on the gas and yanked the steering wheel to the right, taking them off the main road and into the woods. They careened around a tree. Bumped over snow-covered shrubs and debris.

Behind them the truck followed, but it had lost ground.

Up ahead a narrow gully flashed in the headlights. Liz braced herself for the crash. At the last moment, Blake took a hard left, barely missing the gully. Liz slammed her head against the side window, and pain exploded in her eye. The SUV hit the road again and ate up the gravel, snow-packed road at its top speed.

Liz swiveled to see the truck slam on its brakes, barely stopping in time to avoid crashing into the ditch. She let out a relieved breath and turned to face forward. She put a hand to her eyebrow and felt dampness. She dug a tissue out of her pocket and held it to the stinging cut to mop up the blood.

Blake called Nathanial and told him about the truck. After he hung up, he glanced her way. "You okay?"

She nodded. "Just rattled."

He frowned. "You're hurt."

The concern in his tone brought tears to her eyes and heightened the pain. "I hit my head."

"You're bleeding."

She blinked up at him. "Yes, Captain Obvious."

He snorted out a chuckle. "Sorry."

Glad to know he had some semblance of a sense of humor hidden inside him, she tried to relax, but her tension didn't ease until Blake pulled to the curb by Niagara's general hospital twenty minutes later. He jumped out of the SUV and came around to her door. He helped her out, then tucked her at his side. They walked into the emergency waiting area.

"I need help here," he said, taking out his badge and showing it to the nurses and orderlies. "Now."

A nurse hurried to their side, her gaze flitting over the bloodied tissue Liz was pressing against her eyebrow. "Follow me." The nurse guided them toward a curtained room. "A doctor will be with you shortly."

"I can't believe this," Blake muttered. "I promised I'd keep you safe."

His distress tugged at her, making her heart hurt for him. He took on too much blame for things that he had no control over. "It's okay. You got me here safely. You rescued my sister. You're my hero."

He paled and stared at her as if she'd said something horrible. "I need to find Drew. I'll have a patrol officer guard the ER." He brusquely pushed aside the curtain and had to sidestep around the doctor on his way out.

Liz stared after him, hurt and confused. What had she said to send him running away?

You're my hero.

Blake ran a hand through his hair as he leaned against the wall outside of the hospital's emergency room entrance.

No. He wasn't anyone's hero.

From the beginning he'd been using Liz and her sister's kidnapping to bring down Santini.

The fact he was fast falling in love with Liz was a colossal mistake. She'd been hurt on his watch, and that was an even bigger blunder. One he wouldn't ever forgive himself for.

He'd lost Liam because he'd been late providing backup and now he'd let harm befall Liz.

His hands fisted. He'd been so focused on Santini, he'd overlooked the other man who wanted the necklace. Ken. He'd had the IBETs technician run a background check on the man. Kenneth Onega—his real name— was a US citizen hailing from Miami, Florida.

The local law enforcement there had a thick file on him. According to the Miami-Dade County police chief, Ken was a small-time fish looking to swim with the sharks. They'd had intel that he had been trying to muscle in on Santini's operation but with no success.

Blake ground his jaw together, making his head ache. Ken had made a mistake by coming after Liz. Though why he was targeting her didn't make sense...unless he thought she had the necklace. She didn't. Blake did. It was still nestled in his pocket.

Pushing away from the wall, Blake's gaze roamed over the parking lot and faltered on a familiar pickup truck.

A cold knot formed in his chest.

Ken was here at the hospital. And Blake had left Liz alone.

* * *

"In a few days, you'll be good as new," the emergency room doctor said with confidence ringing in his tone.

Liz was thankful she'd only suffered a cut that hadn't needed stitches, just a butterfly bandage. Her head still throbbed, but the doctor had given her some pain reliever. She hoped it would kick in soon. "Thank you, Doctor."

"You were asking about your sister," the doctor said. "She's in a private room on the third floor. Room 302."

"She was admitted?"

"We gave her a sedative to calm her," he said with a rueful twist of his lips. "She was quite upset."

Liz could imagine. Her sister was overly dramatic in the best of circumstances. No doubt Jillian had the hospital staff terrorized with her demands and hysterics.

"I appreciate your help, Doctor." Liz slid off the exam table.

"Of course. The discharge nurse will have you sign some paperwork before you can go see your sister."

As she waited for the nurse, she called Blake but it went straight to voice mail. "It's me, Liz." She cringed. As if he wouldn't recognize her voice? "I'm done here with the doctor. After I sign my discharge papers I'm heading up to the third floor. Jillian's in room three-o-two." She clicked off just as the same nurse who'd admitted her walked over with her discharge papers.

She signed the required documents, then went to the emergency waiting area but didn't see Blake. He'd said Drew and Sami were with her sister, so it stood to reason Blake had gone upstairs. Instead of the elevator she took the stairs to the third floor and passed the nurses' station without stopping to check in.

A uniformed guard sat outside her sister's room. He nodded to her. "Miss Cantrell, you may go in."

"How…?"

"The Kellys showed me a picture of you," the officer said with a smile. "They went in search of food. They'll be back shortly."

Grateful to Sami and Drew, Liz thanked the officer, then took a fortifying breath before pushing the door open. She braced herself for whatever mood she'd find her sister in. Would she be hysterical? Or weepy? Or giddy with relief?

Jillian lay asleep in the bed. Okay, exhausted. That stood to reason. Liz's own fatigue made itself known. Her limbs felt heavy and she couldn't stifle a sudden yawn as she moved to her sister's bedside.

Jillian's blond hair fanned over the pillow. A bruise darkened the pale skin near her temple. She looked so young and vulnerable lying there with the blankets pulled up to her chin.

"Ah, Jillian," Liz whispered with an ache in her throat. She sat in the chair beside the bed and bowed her head. She praised God they'd both made it through the past week in one piece. She prayed for wisdom and guidance. But mostly she prayed for strength to let go of her love for Blake.

A noise brought Liz's gaze to the door. Maybe Sami and Drew were relieving the officer. She rose and walked to the door just as two men stepped inside the room. She collided with a skinny man, who grabbed her with bony fingers wrapped around her arms, forcing her to stop. She'd never seen him in her life. He had thin features that bordered on gaunt. He was dressed in a dark hoodie that covered his head and hung on his lean frame.

She glanced to the side to find Ken standing there with a smirk on his face. Her breath caught and held. What was he doing here? How had he found them? "How did you get in here?"

"Let's just say the guard is taking a siesta in the supply closet," Ken answered.

She swallowed back a lump of fear. Both men carried guns.

"Where's the necklace?" Ken's harsh tone echoed in through the stillness of the hospital room.

What? Why did he think she had it? "The police have it." She kept her voice low, praying the men wouldn't awaken her sister. She'd had enough trauma to last a lifetime.

Ken glanced at his skinny cohort who shook his head. Ken's lip thinned. "The Niagara police don't have it. My guess is your boyfriend does. Where is he?"

"Boyfriend?" Liz frowned at the man. Obviously he meant Blake. And how did he know that the local police didn't have the necklace? "Agent Fallon will be here any second." At least she prayed so.

Ken grabbed Liz and hauled up her against him. She let out a small yelp. He smelled of cigars and alcohol. Her stomach turned with distaste. He pressed the gun into her side.

"Make one wrong move, and you're dead." His gaze flicked over Jillian. "And then she'll be next."

ELEVEN

Liz swallowed back the terror bubbling up inside of her. She couldn't let them hurt Jillian. Not after all she'd suffered to rescue her and bring her to safety. "No, please."

"Then you better cooperate with us," Ken hissed. "Otherwise, you're both dead."

The world dimmed into one horrific thought—what if she never saw Blake again. Her breathing turned shallow. Fearing Ken would make good his threat to kill them both, she nodded, willing to do whatever necessary to survive.

"Good." Ken jerked his chin toward the door. "Come on, let's go find your boyfriend."

She went with them down the corridor. As they passed the nurses' station, Liz met the gaze of the woman behind the desk. Liz tried to convey her panic and mouthed, *help*. The women's eyes widened and she nodded.

Then Ken shoved Liz inside the elevator. She pressed herself into the corner and fought the smothering sensation threatening to bring her to her knees. Now was not the time to give in to her claustrophobia. After having braved the tunnels, she could manage the hospital's elevator. She had to. Ken dug his fingers into her arm. Gritting her teeth against the panic rising up, she silently prayed. After having survived Santini, would her life now end with Ken? How was that even possible?

They rode down to the main floor. When the doors opened, they were met by Blake, Sami and Drew. Their guns were drawn and aimed at them.

Ken's buddy flattened himself to the side of the elevator car while Ken hid behind Liz. His gun was still jammed into her ribs. "Out of the way or I'll kill her."

"You'll be dead before you can pull the trigger," Blake said, his voice strangely calm yet menacing.

Ken ducked even more behind Liz. "I don't believe you'll risk her life."

Liz kept her gaze on Blake. He would get her out of this just as he had the other times her life was in danger. She trusted him implicitly.

Blake lowered the barrel of his gun and backed up. "Step out of the elevator."

Peeking over her shoulder, Ken said, "You toss me the necklace first."

Reaching into his pocket, Blake brought out the string of uncut diamonds. "I'll give them to you once you let her go."

Ken swore and tightened his hold on Liz, his fingers bruising her flesh. "That's not how this works." He kept her in front of him as he pushed her out of the elevator while continuing to use her as a shield. "Everyone stay back," Ken shouted.

He pressed the business end of his pistol to her head just below the bandage covering the wound she'd suffered earlier when she'd smacked her head against the window.

Liz's breath turned erratic. She tried to think of how she could help Blake get her out of this situation, but her mind refused to work. Dots danced at the edges of her mind. She fought to focus, refusing to give in to the terror wanting to take hold of her.

"Yeah, stay back," Ken's cohort echoed as he followed behind Ken.

Ken swiveled so that he dragged her backward away from Blake. People scurried out of their way.

Blake moved with them. The determination in his dark eyes was unmistakable. Liz kept her attention on him, rather than on the man holding a gun to her head.

"Don't come any closer or she's dead!" Ken yelled and pressed the gun harder into her temple. She winced. They were at the hospital exit.

Ken's crony pushed open the door. "Forget the necklace. Let's go while we can."

"She's coming with us," Ken said and tugged her toward the open door.

Panic seized her. There was no way she was going with Ken. Whether he killed her here on the spot or at some other location, he would kill her. She knew that in the depths of her soul. She'd die alone only to have her body discovered when the weather thawed the frozen ground.

And she would never get to tell Blake she loved him. Her heart clenched. No. No. No.

She said a prayer and then set her jaw with resolve.

She'd escaped from Ken before, she'd do it again. Not allowing the fear shredding through her to take hold, she rammed her elbow into his gut and at the same time she reared her head back to ram her skull into his nose. She heard the crunch of bone breaking. The hand holding the gun swung away from her.

"Down!"

She heard Blake's cry. It took only a second for her to process his meaning. She went limp. Ken couldn't hold her weight while trying to stop the blood squirting from his nose. She dropped to the ground in a heap. The loud retort of a gun reverberated through her head. Her ears throbbed and the world became muted. But she felt no pain. Ken fell next to her with a dull thud. A crimson stain spread across his shoulder. He'd been shot.

Drew sprinted out the door after the other man who'd cursed, then raced away, leaving his friend behind to face his fate. Sami kicked Ken's gun out of his reach and then hovered over him, her pistol aimed at his forehead.

Strong arms gathered Liz close. She blinked as Blake's face came into focus. She clutched his broad shoulders.

It was over.

She saw Blake's lips move but his voice didn't penetrate the ringing in her head. He lifted her into his arms and carried her back to her sister's room.

* * *

Blake watched the two sisters reunite. Jillian had awoken and now clung to Liz.

His heart swelled with gratitude to God above for allowing this happy reunion. It could have just as easily gone so bad. Ken could've made good on his threat to kill Liz. Santini could've killed both women along the way.

An insidious feeling of helplessness lingered, making Blake aware of how close he'd come to losing the only woman he'd ever truly loved. A fate he had no idea how to deal with. He could face down criminals with guns and explosives, but admitting to his feelings, telling Liz how he felt, had him in a cold sweat.

"Hey." Nathanial clapped him on the back. "Drew and Sami are sticking close to Ken. The bullet was a through and through. Nice shooting, by the way."

"Thanks," Blake murmured, drawing Nathanial out of the room and into the hallway where they wouldn't disturb the Cantrell sisters.

He'd had no time to think, let alone plan a clean shot that would render Ken powerless but wouldn't kill him. Blake had reacted in the split second it had taken his mind to process the horror of seeing the barrel of the gun pressed to Liz's head. His insides had quaked, and his heart had pounded with fear, which still pulsed through his veins.

That she'd responded swiftly to his shouted demand, recognizing what he was asking of her, made his heart expand with pride and love. When it counted the most, she'd trusted him without question.

"Why don't you stay here with Liz and Jillian? Liz will need to give a statement and I'm sure she would appreciate a friendly face," Nathanial said with a knowing look that punched Blake in the solar plexus.

Did Nathanial know Blake had fallen in love with Liz? Were Blake's feelings so transparent? How had Blake let himself fall for her in the first place?

As much as Blake would like to stick close to Liz, he knew he shouldn't. Couldn't. Though this situation had ended in the best possible way, the torment he'd experienced in those horrifying moments when he'd had no control over the situation had left an indelible impression. Even now he worried about Liz. Would she make it home safely? Would she have nightmares after this ordeal?

Who would be there to comfort her?

A desperate feeling clutched at him because he knew it wouldn't be him. He didn't like the feeling of desperation one bit. It left him too vulnerable, too much at the mercy of someone else, despite the love that had taken root deep in his heart for Liz.

He had to do the only thing he could to protect himself. Let her go. "No. I'm needed at the station to process Santini. This started and ends with him."

The look Nathanial gave him spoke volumes. The Canada Border Services officer thought he was nuts.

Maybe Blake *was* crazy. But he'd rather not feel than ever go through the torture again of feeling so weak.

"You'll get the sisters safely back to the States?" Blake asked, needing to make sure that someone Liz knew and trusted would take care of her.

"Of course, but I think you should do it," Nathanial said. "Liz will want you to."

"I can't," Blake replied.

Nathanial shook his head. "What is it with you? Are you afraid you'll actually feel something?"

Anger reared up as a defense against Nathanial's well-placed dart to his heart. He did feel, and that was the problem.

His father had lamented often enough that emotions made men weak. He'd learned the truth of his father's belief the hard way. With Sarah. Her lies had cut him to the quick and slashed deep into his heart.

And despite what he'd learned from Liz about unconditional love, regarding the difference between being in a relationship and being relational, he couldn't change now. He didn't know how. All he knew how to be was relational. That he was failing her in a different way dug deep but it was a wound he'd have to live with.

Better that than hurting her later on.

In order to maintain the friendship and the working camaraderie he had with the Canadian, Blake chose to ignore Nathanial's questions. "I'll see you later. I'm sure Deputy Director Moore will want a briefing as soon as Santini is processed and on his way to the US."

The disappointment in Nathanial's eyes as he turned away hounded Blake all the way to the Niagara Regional Police station. At the station he made sure Santini was securely locked up in a cell.

Because Santini, Travis and Ken were citizens of the United States, each man would be tried in a US Federal Court. The extradition treaty between the two countries would be honored by the Canadian government. Blake figured the Canadians didn't want the headache of trying the international criminals.

Blake was shown to a conference room where he started the ball rolling toward extradition by filing the appropriate affidavit, which stated the facts of the case and listed the charges piled sky-high against Santini and the others from smuggling, theft and kidnapping to the premeditated murder of an ICE agent.

Blake wasn't surprised when Drew and Sami appeared in the conference room doorway the following day. As the assistant to the legal attaché for the United States in Canada, Sami would have a hand in the extradition process for the three men.

"Good work yesterday," Drew said. "You brought down Santini just as you'd planned from the beginning. I know you've been after him for a while."

"I have," Blake said. "But until he's secured in a federal penitentiary serving a life sentence, I won't relax."

"Thought you'd want to know," Drew said. "Ken's buddy Daniel Shepherd is from Niagara and will be facing charges here. He has a cousin on the police force, which is how he and Ken were able to evade capture as well as keep tabs on the necklace. Needless to say the officer in question will be facing charges."

"That's good to know," Blake said.

"Jillian was released from the hospital last night," Sami interjected. "She and Liz are at the airport. Their flight leaves in a few hours."

A knot formed in Blake's gut. His lungs grew tight. She was returning home. He knew she would. He wanted her to, but the reality of Liz leaving still affected him in ways he'd rather not feel.

"Liz asked about you. She was wondering if she'd be able to talk to you before they left." Sami narrowed her blue eyes. "You are going to see them off, right?"

Uncomfortable beneath her intense stare, he tugged at the collar of his shirt. "No. I need to stay here. As soon as the extradition is approved, I want to move Santini."

Drew arched an eyebrow. "That's not your jurisdiction. We'll wait here for the US Marshals Service to arrive and escort Santini and the others back to the US."

"I know the protocol. But I don't trust Santini not to have something up his sleeve. He's too cunning, too well versed in law enforcement procedures not to have an escape plan," Blake informed them. "I need to be there to avert any attempt at getting away from the marshals."

Sami put a hand on his arm. "Trust me, I understand. You've been chasing him so long it's become personal."

"It wasn't the chase that made it personal, it was Liam's death," he corrected her.

"Yes. I get it. For me it was my best friend's death that made catching Birdman personal." There was no mistaking the empathy in her eyes. "I wouldn't give up, and I was determined to bring him down on my own." She cast a loving glance to Drew. "But sometimes you need to step back and allow others to take the lead."

Though Blake understood and would even agree under different circumstances, he couldn't back off now. He had to see this through.

"Look, Blake," Sami said, her voice hard-edged. "If you don't say goodbye to Liz, you'll never have closure."

"Who says I need closure?"

Sami glared at him. "You can't kid a kidder. You've got it bad for Liz. And she for you. If you don't want to pursue it, then don't, but at least give her closure if you don't want it for yourself. You owe her that."

"I don't owe anyone anything." He couldn't stop the defensive tone. "I kept my promises to Liz. Santini is in jail. Her sister has been freed, and they are both safe. There's nothing more for me to do."

With great effort, Sami visibly reined in her temper. "I misspoke. The fair thing would be for you to say goodbye."

Blake looked to Drew for help. The big Canadian spread his hands wide. "I have to agree with my wife, and not just because she's my wife."

Running a nervous hand through his hair, Blake contemplated what saying goodbye to Liz would be like. Uncomfortable. Hard. Emotional. His gut clenched, and acid burned his throat. An image of her pretty blue-green eyes and her lush mouth flittered across his mind.

Maybe the only way, the sane way, to get

her out of his head and keep her out was to do as Sami suggested and go to the airport to say goodbye.

"You'll stay here?" he asked the couple.

"Yes," Drew answered. "If anything note-worthy happens we'll contact you."

Sami's smile smacked of triumph and sad-ness. "You'll be glad in the long run that you stepped up and said farewell, Blake." She leaned against her husband. "It's the only way either one of you will be able to move forward."

Move forward. He used to know what that looked like. But now… He could only hope Sami was right.

And that he wasn't making a big mistake.

Liz sat on the uncomfortable plastic chair in the Buffalo Niagara International Airport. She should be relieved that the horrible night-mare she and her sister had found themselves in was over. Her sister was safe. Her kidnap-per was behind bars. Even the man who'd threatened to kill Liz was in police custody. As was Travis, the man who'd started it all with his thievery.

Yesterday, after Nathanial had taken Liz and Jillian back to the hotel where Jillian's belongings were, Liz had hoped Blake would show up. He hadn't. She'd thought maybe he'd be the one to bring her clothes and suitcase from the condo, but it had been the Kellys instead.

Though she was glad to see Drew and Sami and to thank them for all they had done, Liz had been crushed that Blake hadn't come to see her. She held out hope he'd be the one to take them to the airport the next morning, but it had been the Kellys again.

When Liz had asked about Blake, Sami had seemed surprised Blake hadn't already been to the hotel. Sami had tried to assure her Blake was busy processing Santini and the others. It seemed plausible. Probable. But it still hurt that Blake had stayed away.

The Kellys had made sure Liz and Jillian had a police escort across the border to the airport. And now here she sat, waiting to go home. Yet Liz wasn't happy. Not even close.

Sure, she and her sister were now free to return home. Granted, Jillian was returning brokenhearted. She'd been on her honeymoon, but her new husband was now sitting in jail. Jillian faced the decision whether to remain married to him or not. They'd been raised to believe marriage was forever.

How did Jillian stay true to her beliefs when the person she'd promised herself to turned out not to be the person she'd thought she'd married? Whatever her decision, Liz would support her sister. They'd been through too much together for her not to stand by her.

They'd left Canada behind and with it the memories of the past week.

Only the thought of not seeing Blake again ate away at Liz. She kept telling herself it was for the best. She told herself she'd get over him. But the truth was she loved Blake. She just didn't know what to do about it.

Beside her Jillian napped, leaning forward with her arms crossed over her luggage and her tearstained cheek resting on her forearms. She looked so young and vulnerable. Protectiveness rose in Liz as it always did when it came to her little sister. Though three years separated them, at times it felt more like twenty.

Who watches out for you and your needs? Blake's words spoken on the first night echoed through her head, stirring up confusing thoughts and emotions.

She told herself she didn't need anyone taking care of her. She was doing just fine on her own. And once she returned home, life would go back to normal. She wanted normal. Quiet. Uneventful.

But the thudding in her heart claimed she was fooling herself. She loved Blake. But surely time and distance would diminish the pain of not having that love returned?

"Liz."

As if her thoughts had conjured him up, she jerked her attention to the man towering over her. Blake. Her heart stalled, then thumped an erratic beat within her chest, and her insides went gooey. She was in trouble. So much trouble.

And she had no idea what to do about it.

TWELVE

Blake had come to the airport to tell Liz goodbye. Sami had said it was the fair thing to do. For some reason that had sounded like a good idea then, but now the words were lodged in his chest, held captive by his heart. Her sister rested beside her, but his focus was solely on Liz. He stood there mute, drinking her in as if he was in the desert and she was the only source of sustenance he needed or craved.

She looked so weary yet so heartbreakingly pretty. Her honey-blond hair was pulled to one side, spilling over her shoulder in a low ponytail. The emerald-colored sweater and black jeans accentuated her curves. She had no makeup on. She didn't need any. She had a natural beauty that didn't require any enhancing.

Her sea-colored eyes were wide and held

a mix of surprise, wariness and yearning, which stirred answering emotions within him. He took in a stuttering breath and tried to find his voice.

She rose and spoke before he could utter a word. "I didn't think you'd come."

The softly spoken statement held no accusation or blame, just a wistfulness that pierced him, reminding him of the reasons he was there. To bring closure to their...the word *relationship* rang through his head.

He forced the words out before he lost his nerve and gave in to the thrumming attraction and affection—love—expanding within his heart. "I came to say goodbye."

A flash of disappointment in her lovely eyes had him regretting the words. He never was so wishy-washy. He always knew his own mind. His own heart. He was doing the right thing by severing whatever it was that had started between them.

She glanced away for a moment. When she returned her attention to him, the disappointment was nowhere to be found in her eyes. Now she wore a polite mask that didn't settle well with him.

"I appreciate that," she said. "Goodbye,

Blake. I will always be grateful to you for saving my sister." She smiled. "And me."

He didn't like that she always put her sister before herself. Over the past week he had seen her put others before herself and her own safety time and time again. He wished he could make her see how special and wonderful she was, how much she had to offer the world.

However, it wasn't his place to do that, not if he wanted to end things between them now.

But he didn't want to walk away. Not yet. He reached for her hand, half-afraid she'd refuse to let him touch her. She willingly slipped her small, delicate hand into his. It wasn't enough. He pulled her to him so that he could encircle her with his arms. She leaned back to stare up at him with a question in her eyes. He didn't have an answer as to why he was doing this. He just knew if he didn't kiss her, he'd never be able to get her out of his mind, out of his heart.

He dipped his head, hovering over her lush mouth, waiting for her permission. He held his breath, hoping she wanted this as much as he did. She made a soft little sound in her throat and rose on her toes to close the gap between them and fitted her mouth to his.

Sensation exploded through his system. He embraced her tighter, drawing her into him as if he could absorb her.

The world around them faded to white noise. It didn't matter that they were surrounded by people or that any second her plane would board and he'd have to face the reality of his life without her.

For this moment, this time in space, they were two halves of a whole. He deepened the kiss, taking all she offered and giving all he had, knowing it would never be enough. He'd made a tactical error. Kissing her had been the biggest blunder ever because he never wanted to let her go.

"Lizzie," Jillian's voice intruded. "Lizzie, they called for our plane to board."

Liz eased back, breaking the contact. She placed a hand over his heart. Tears glistened in her eyes. "Goodbye, Blake."

She disengaged from him, grabbed her suitcase and walked away.

He stared after her, unable to move, to think. Suddenly his life seemed so empty. He felt so alone.

Before she headed down the Jetway, she paused and turned to wave.

He couldn't bring himself to wave back, to

finalize this moment. His heart felt as frozen as the water of Niagara Falls.

Her hand dropped slowly to her side, an expression of gut-wrenching agony stole over her lovely face.

Then she disappeared out of view. The world around him rushed in, the chaos and noise making his head pound and his heart ache.

This was his choice. The only choice he could make. It was time to put the memory of Liz in a box in his heart. He had work to do. More smugglers, murderers and thieves to bring to justice.

His job was his life.

But the thought didn't hold the same amount of conviction that it had before he'd met Liz.

Liz sat in the aisle seat on the plane bound for South Carolina, her fingers digging into the armrests and her heart thudding wildly in her chest. Jillian sat next to her, calmly flipping through a magazine. Liz was glad Jillian wasn't in a chatty mood for once.

Liz needed some time to come to grips with what had just happened before she'd boarded the plane. Blake had shown up out of the blue. She'd had no indication he would see them off so she hadn't been prepared to find him standing there looking so handsome and uncertain.

She wasn't sure why he'd arrived but was glad he had. And even more glad that he'd initiated a kiss. She'd wanted to kiss him for the longest time. That the kiss was a goodbye kiss didn't diminish its power or lingering affect.

Wow. That's the only word she could think of to describe how it had felt to be within Blake's embrace. Sure, he'd put his arm around her before, but she'd not been able to really relish the other times because of the underscoring danger chasing after her.

Suddenly she missed Blake so much. Would she ever see him again?

Doubtful.

A tear slipped unbidden down her cheek. She wiped it away, hoping no one noticed.

"Lizzie, what's wrong?"

Jillian's softly asked question made the tears fall faster. Pressing the heels of her hands to her eyes, Liz fought to stop the flow of unhappiness leaking down her face. "I'm fine."

Jillian harrumphed. "Right. Like you'd ever

let me get away with a nonanswer like that. What gives?"

Dropping her hands from her face and smoothing her palms over her thighs, Liz tried to hedge. "It's all catching up to me. Everything we've been through this past week." She lowered her voice. "You were the one who was kidnapped for days. How are you doing?"

Huffing out a little sigh, Jillian said, "Okay. I miss Travis."

Liz covered Jillian's hand with her own. "I'm so sorry things turned out badly." It wasn't in Liz's nature to gloat that she'd been right about Travis, so she kept the thought to herself.

"I should have listened to you," Jillian admitted. "Maybe if Travis and I had slowed our relationship down none of this would have happened."

She clamped her teeth together to keep from pointing out that nothing would have changed the fact that Travis was a criminal. Pure and simple.

"I know what you're thinking," Jillian's voice took on a peevish tone that grated on Liz. "You think Travis is a bad man because of what he did."

"And you don't?"

Jillian shook her head. "No. He's made some really bad choices, but he's not a bad person."

Remembering the way Travis had shielded her from Ken, Liz had to concede that point. "No, he's not a totally bad person."

"He loves me," Jillian stated. "And I love him."

"But he's in jail. And will be for a long time."

"And I'll be there when he gets out."

Liz stared at Jillian, noting the determination in her clear blue eyes. But also seeing the black and blue skin over her cheek where Santini had hit her. Liz's fingers curled with suppressed anger. "That will be a hard path to take."

"I know." Jillian lifted her chin. "But it will be worth it. Our love is worth fighting for."

Liz's heart spasmed in her chest. Her sister was so brave and yet so reckless. How could she stay true to a man who'd put her life in jeopardy? Would her and Travis's love withstand the pressure of a jail sentence and then the life that would come after he was out? He'd always have a criminal record.

Was Jillian's love enough to change Travis's ways?

Liz prayed it would be enough for Jillian's sake. Even as longing hit her hard.

She wanted to have a love like that, a love worth fighting for. She wanted that with Blake. Fresh tears pricked her eyes. But there was too much separating them. His job. Her life on Hilton Head Island. His need to be free from entanglements. Her fear of losing herself.

Jillian squeezed her hand. "Hey, Lizzie. Please tell me what has you so upset."

"I don't want to burden you with my troubles," Liz said.

"Oh, please," Jillian huffed. "I burden you all the time. You're due. For once let me be the strong one."

Needing to talk about it, Liz gave in. "I—" Saying the words out loud was harder than she'd imagined. "I love Blake."

A wide grin spread over her sister's face. "I knew it."

"Did not."

"Oh, yeah." Jillian wagged her eyebrows. "You don't kiss someone like you did back at the airport if you aren't in love with them."

"I wouldn't know," Liz said. "It's been a long time since anyone has wanted to kiss me."

Jillian made a raspberry sound. "That's because you don't let anyone get close enough for you to find out if they want to kiss you."

"That's not true." Though Liz knew what her sister said was exactly true. "Mostly, not true."

"Name the last time you went on a date," Jillian challenged.

Liz frowned and stared at the back of the tray table. She didn't want to admit it had been years since she'd gone on a bonafide date. "It doesn't matter. He said goodbye. There was no 'I'll see you soon' or anything like that."

"Well, did you ask if you could see him again?"

"No." And she never would. It was better to keep the break clean. Better to do it before her heart was any more involved than it already was.

"You should tell him how you feel," Jillian advised.

The very idea made her heart pound. "It wouldn't work out."

"Why not?"

"He has a risky job that keeps him moving from place to place. My life is on the island. Someone has to manage the shop." She didn't understand the resentment bubbling up inside. She liked managing the shop; she enjoyed her quiet, uneventful life on Hilton Head Island. Only the thought of never seeing Blake again made the future appear dull and lifeless.

"I could manage the shop."

Liz hid a smile as love for her sister filled her to the brim. "The point is Blake's life and mine wouldn't mesh." How could they?

"They would if you let them." Jillian snapped open her magazine. "You're making up excuses."

Stung by that pronouncement, Liz couldn't keep the defensiveness from her voice. "I'm not like you, Jillian. I can't just go with every whim I feel."

Jillian arched an eyebrow. "Oh, well if what you feel for Blake is just a whim..."

Liz frowned; that wasn't at all what she'd meant. "It's not a whim. It's just..."

"You're making a mistake." Jillian closed the magazine and took Liz's hand. Suddenly Jillian seemed older and wiser than she'd ever had. "Sometimes in life you have to take a leap of faith. It would be good for you to step out of the bubble you've insulated yourself in and live a little."

More defensiveness rose along with some

indignation. "Hey, I did step way out of my comfort zone to help you."

Tenderness softened Jillian's gaze. "To which I'm eternally grateful." She released Liz's hand. "It's time I start taking more responsibility for my life."

Surprised but glad to hear it, Liz said, "I'm proud of you Jillian."

"Thanks. I want to enroll in some business classes so I can help run the store. Or maybe start my own business with my art."

Either were steps in the right direction. Her baby sister was growing up. "I think that's a fabulous idea."

"I just hope you'll stop hiding in the shop," Jillian said. "It's time for you to have a life of your own, Lizzie."

Unnerved to realize her baby sister had grown up and didn't need her the way she had before, Liz mulled over her sister's surprisingly sound words.

But deep in her heart she knew it was too late for her and Blake.

And the knowledge left her miserable.

Two weeks later, Liz stepped into the dining room of the apartment she and Jillian shared over the family antique store to find

Jillian had her craft box out and the dining table covered in glitter and glue and scraps of paper.

Jillian had tamed her hair back with a red ribbon. Her peaches-and-cream skin was scrubbed clean. No traces of the bruises she'd suffered at the hands of Santini remained. She looked young and fresh.

She'd surprised Liz by actually doing as she'd said she would on the plane. Jillian had enrolled in some online business classes and Liz was teaching her the ins and outs of the antique shop.

They would head to the early service at the community church. Liz had thrown herself into volunteering more at church as a way to keep her time occupied. Because any time she found herself idle, thoughts of Blake would drift through her mind. The kiss they shared had left a tiny piece of hope in her heart that maybe he felt something more for her than just friendship or obligation. And that hope continually sent her spiraling into a depression that she feared she'd never shake.

Liz grabbed a cup for coffee. "What are you doing?"

Jillian held up the card she was making.

"It's for Travis. You know Valentine's Day is coming up."

Right. A day for couples. She poured coffee into her cup and noticed her hands shook.

"You should send Blake a card," Jillian said.

The thought was like a spear to her heart. She hadn't heard anything from him these past weeks and didn't expect to. But she still jumped a bit every time the phone rang, hoping that maybe he'd call just to check on her. Silly. He was off on some assignment, protecting the country from bad guys doing bad things. The last thing on his mind was her. And she'd be all kinds of a fool to think otherwise. Wouldn't she be?

"I'm not creative like you are," Liz said.

"Then buy a card."

She made it sound so simple. There was nothing simple about Liz's feelings for Blake. She hadn't wanted to get involved with him because she'd feared losing herself to him but she was losing herself anyway. Every day she felt less like herself. Every day she slipped deeper into a thick abyss of discontentment.

Jillian came to her side and put an arm around her waist. Dropping her head on Liz's shoulder, she said, "I'm worried about you."

Picking up the edges of her composure, she put on a brave smile. "No need to be."

Jillian raised her head and gave Liz a disbelieving look. "Right. You're mopey and irritable. You need to snap out of it."

Liz sighed, knowing she was right. "I would if I could."

"Send Blake a note. Ask him to dinner on Valentine's Day. If he doesn't answer or doesn't show then you can write him off. And maybe get on with your life."

"I'm not brave like you," Liz whispered past the constriction in her throat. Not when it came to matters of the heart.

Jillian pursed her lips. "You are the bravest person I've ever met. Just not when it comes to love." She shrugged. "It's your life. I'm going to go get ready for church." She skipped out of the room as if she was ten rather than twenty-three.

Going to the table, Liz contemplated what she should do. She did need to move on with her life. She felt stuck, in limbo, waiting for something to happen that wouldn't unless she was fearless enough to initiate it. Picking up a sheet of cardstock, she made a decision. She would invite Blake to come to the island for a Valentine's Day dinner. And if he rejected her offer then she'd be able to kill that speck of hope once and for all.

Blake sat in his usual seat around the large table and stared out the window of the conference room in Washington, DC. The view of the Washington Monument in the distance had always made him feel patriotic.

But lately, irritation seemed to be the only thing he could feel.

He'd been called to the Homeland Security office for a meeting with the US personnel side of the various IBETs members. Every few months they'd gather to debrief on the program, looking for ways to improve their effectiveness. Usually Blake had plenty of ideas and opinions.

But not today. The Valentine's Day card in his pocket burned clean through his shirt to brand his skin.

It had arrived two days ago. He still didn't know what to make of it. Nor did he know if he wanted to respond. And the indecision was wreaking havoc on his psyche.

The handmade card was not just a greeting but also an invitation. A Valentine's Day dinner invitation. From Liz. Her sweet face danced through his mind, and his heart kicked into high gear demanding he acknowledge that he couldn't stop thinking about her. Couldn't stop dreaming of being with her, kissing her again. Holding her close, hearing her voice, her laugh.

For a man who didn't do emotions, that was all he seemed to be made of these days. A hot, messy glob of emotion.

His dad would have a field day of mockery if Blake ever admitted he'd fallen head over heels in love with a woman who made him *feel*.

"Hey, Blake. Earth to Blake."

He snapped his attention to the man seated across the table from him. "What!"

"Whoa!" US Border Patrol agent Jeff Steele, raised his hand. "Dude, what's up with you?"

"Nothing." Thankfully they were the only two in the room at the moment.

Blake better get his head back in the game before the other agents and officers, including the deputy director, joined them.

Jeff raised an eyebrow. "Something."

He eyed the agent with interest. Steele had been married a little over a year now to a woman he'd met while on an assignment in northern Washington state. She was a doctor, a biologist actually. Together they'd brought down an illegal marijuana grower and human trafficker. "How did you know you loved Tessa?"

A slow grin spread over Jeff's face. "Ah, I see. You're in love, and you're not sure what to do about it."

Blake grunted. "Something like that. So? You gonna answer the question?"

Jeff stroked his chin. "Well, I fell in love long before I decided to do something about it."

"Yeah?" Blake straightened in his seat, his curiosity piqued.

"Let me put it this way, I didn't believe in love until I was hit with it square in the heart." Jeff smiled. "I came to a point where I knew I couldn't live without her in my life. And that, brother, is the true test. Living without Tessa was miserable. I couldn't concentrate or barely think. Every moment apart was torture."

"Hmmm," Blake considered his words. His heartbeat sped up. He felt as if he was on the top of an iceberg and any second he'd fall off. "How long did that take?"

"Not long." Jeff sat back. "Not long at all."

They were interrupted by the arrival of the others. Nathanial took the seat next to him.

Jeff leaned forward to say. "What do you think of the mighty Fallon falling in love?"

Blake groaned. Great. Nathanial would have a field day with this information.

Nathanial grinned from ear to ear. "Well, well. This is news. Have to say I'm glad you've finally come to your senses."

Had he come to his senses? It was either that or he'd lost his mind.

All through the meeting, Blake had to force himself to concentrate on the proceedings. Questions rolled around inside his head and his heart. Could he live without Liz? Did he want to?

Would loving her make him weak? Or would she be a source of strength like nothing else in his life?

By the time the meeting concluded, he'd come to a decision. He booked himself on the next flight out of Washington Dulles International Airport for South Carolina and to the resort island home of the woman he loved.

Nervous flutters danced in the pit of Liz's tummy as she waited inside Hilton Head Island's most posh restaurant. The hostess had seated her ten minutes ago. It would be another ten minutes before the time she'd told

Blake to arrive. Would he show up? Or would
she sit here alone, making a fool of herself?

She wiped her damp palms on the white
napkin covering her lap. The red velvet dress
Jillian had insisted on buying her hugged
her like a second skin. Jillian had worked
her wonders on Liz's limp hair, making the
strands shine and adding a touch of bling in
the form of clips holding her hair back from
her face. Liz had allowed her sister to do her
makeup with instructions to go light and was
surprised when she'd looked in the mirror. Jillian really was good with makeup.

But was it all for nothing?

She took a drink of water to soothe the
ache in her throat.

The glow of the votive candle on the table
danced as someone came up to the table. Expecting the waitress wanting to take her order
again, Liz glanced up. Her breath stalled at
the sight of the handsome man regarding her
with a tender smile.

"You're here," she breathed out, hardly dar-
ing to believe Blake had actually showed.
He'd received her card and accepted her invitation to dinner.

"I'm here." He held out his hand. He looked
sharp in a navy pinstripe suit with a red tie.

Though he was dressed much as he'd been when they'd first met, she didn't view him the same at all. Back then he'd been imposing, striking fear in her. A cold threat blocking her rescue of her sister.

Now he was a man who represented respect and trust and honor. A man she admired and loved. A man who'd kept his promises. Gone was the hard and intimidating man she'd been afraid of. Now he was everything good and right in her world.

She was powerless not to slip her hand into his. Setting aside her napkin, she allowed him to draw her to her feet.

From behind his back, he produced her mother's inlaid cedar jewelry box.

She gasped in delight.

"The CI guys picked it up in the tunnel and after they cleared it in evidence, I convinced them to let me take it. I know how important it is to you."

She reverently took the box and clutched it to her heart. "I thought it was lost forever." Tears of gratitude filled her eyes. "How can I ever thank you?"

A slow grin spread across his face. "I'll think of something. May I tell you how beautiful you are?" he murmured with an admiring gleam in his eyes.

A blush flamed in her cheeks. "Yes, please."

"You're stunning." He pulled her close.

It felt amazing to be in his embrace. A place she never wanted to leave.

"Thank you," she dropped her gaze. "You're very kind." She peered up at him through her lashes. "And handsome in your suit."

He lifted her chin with the crook of his finger. "Thank you for reaching out. I'm really happy you did."

Elated to hear his words she thought for sure her feet must be floating ten inches above the ground. "You are?"

He nodded and dipped his head for a tender kiss. His lips were soft, warm, like home. When he pulled away she leaned toward him wanting more.

"We should order," he said, making her aware of the curious stares of the other restaurant patrons.

Heat climbing up her neck, she nodded and sat back in her seat. He sat down across from her and immediately took her hand across the table. "Happy Valentine's Day."

Giddy with delight, she gazed into the eyes

of the man she loved and said, "Happy Valentine's Day to you, too."

He lifted his water goblet. "To us."

She tilted her head as she lifted her glass with her free hand. What did this mean? "Is there an 'us'?"

He set his glass down. Then took her glass and placed it on the table before gathering both of her hands in his.

"I very much want for there to be an 'us.' Don't you?"

The uncertainty in his eyes tugged at her heart. He was as scared of his feelings as she was of her own. Tenderness and affection flooded her. Love overflowed her heart. She leaned toward him. "Yes, I do."

She swallowed back the fear that threatened to keep her words from coming out. Pushing forward she had to jump in with both feet. "These past few weeks without you have been agonizing. Every moment of every day I've wanted to see you, to touch you, to be with you. I don't think I can go on without you because I love you, Blake Fallon."

The admission dislodged something inside of her. She suddenly felt so free, so light without the burden of fear. She didn't have to worry about losing herself to love. With

Blake she'd found herself. "I hope that one day maybe you can love me, too."

A slow smile spread across his handsome face, and his eyes filled with joy. "You have no idea how happy that makes me to hear you say that."

He mirrored her move and leaned closer. Their lips were inches apart. Their gazes locked. "I haven't been able to concentrate or even think from the moment you left me at the airport. I don't want to live without you. I can't live without you. I love you, Liz Cantrell. And I hope one day you'll do me the honor of becoming my wife."

Euphoria, like she'd never known before, had her closing the distance between them for a kiss that she knew cemented their love for each other.

When the kiss ended, she saw the love she felt reflected there in his warm, chocolate gaze. Her heart melted within her chest. "I would be honored to be your wife. To love you, honor you and cherish you all the days of my life.

His boyish grin curled her toes. "Excellent."

She squeezed his hands. "I will live wherever you need to live."

"I only need to be where there's an airport close by."

"There's one close by here," she couldn't keep the lift of hope out of her tone.

He wagged his eyebrows. "I know. When should we do this?"

She grinned back at him. "As soon as we can?"

"Yes, please." He captured her lips again and the world faded to only them and their love.

EPILOGUE

Liz dug her toes into the warm sand and stared out at the beautiful azure blue of Caribbean sea, the water stretching for miles in all directions. The white masts of sailboats provided perspective to delineate the blue-green water from the cloudless blue sky. A salty breeze tickled across her skin and the sun's rays kissed her back, bathing her in a warm glow.

Peace like she'd never known made her muscles languid and her mind free to appreciate the turn of events that had lead her to this moment. As difficult as the ordeal in Niagara Falls had been, what with Jillian being kidnapped and held for ransom, Liz traveling north and working with the IBETs team to rescue her sister and to bring down the criminal mastermind behind the illegal smuggling of contraband between several countries, some really good things had resulted.

Her sister was free and studying business and taking a real interest and responsibility in the antique store. Jillian had even set up a section of the store to display and sell her artwork. She'd decided to honor her marriage vows to Travis and awaited his time in prison to end. Twice a week she made the trek to Edgefield, South Carolina, where Travis was incarcerated in the state's federal penitentiary. Thanks to Blake, the courts had granted Travis's request to do his time as close to Jillian as he could get. In three years he'd be released. Jillian was counting off the days.

Santini and Ken were both in federal prisons in other states. If Liz never saw either of the two men again as long as she lived she'd die happy. And the man who had told Ken the police didn't have the necklace had been arrested as well, along with the dirty Niagara Regional Police officer. A cousin who'd been feeding him information.

Then there was Blake.

Who would have guessed that a stolen necklace of uncut diamonds would bring the most wonderful man into her life? A man more valuable than any jewel could ever be.

That Valentine's Day dinner six months ago had been the beginning of a new life. A life more wondrous than she could ever have imagined. Blake had become a constant in her life and two days ago they'd married before their family and friends. The little community church on Hilton Head Island had been filled to the brim. On his side were his parents, his sister and her family and a whole slew of agents and officers from both the United States and Canada. So many that several had spilled over to her side of the aisle to claim the few remaining seats.

It had seemed as if the whole town had turned out for her wedding. Sheriff Ward had given her away in her father's stead. Jillian had been the perfect matron of honor and Nathanial the best man. The reception had lasted well into the evening, almost making her and Blake late for the flight to their island honeymoon destination.

A shadow passed over her, drawing her attention. Shielding her eyes from the sun, she stared up at the man whom she'd pledged her undying love to.

"What are you doing?" he asked.

"Thinking."

He plopped down in the sand beside her and

kissed her bare shoulder. "Happy thoughts, I hope."

"Yes, very happy."

He stretched out his tanned legs. "You're not worrying about Jillian and the shop are you?"

She laughed. "No. She'll do just fine without me there."

Twirling his fingers into her hair, he said, "Good. Because I don't want to share you with anyone."

"Never?"

He wagged his eyebrows at her. "Well, at least until we have kids."

She giggled at the prospect of filling the cottage they'd purchased on Hilton Head Island, just a few blocks from the shop, with children. Since now Blake was working from home and traveling only when he was on a case, he'd be there to help raise their kids. "I like the sound of that."

"I like this place." He leaned back onto his elbows, turning his handsome face to the sun. "I could get used to the sunshine."

She followed his lead by leaning back and then shifted onto one elbow to face him. "I think we should do this every year."

"Do what?"

She grinned and bumped her shoulder to his. "A yearly honeymoon."

He rolled toward her and propped himself on his elbow. With his finger he drew little circles on her arm. "Our first married tradition."

Love for this man filled her heart to near bursting. "The first of many traditions."

As they kissed, Liz could feel God's smile surround them and she knew without a doubt that their lives, their futures, were in His hands.

* * * * *

Dear Reader,

I hope you enjoyed the journey to Niagara Falls with Liz and Blake. When I first brought ICE agent Blake Fallon onto the page in my July 2015 book *Joint Investigation*, I knew he needed a story of his own. It took me a while to get to know Blake and the pain that he carried. Pairing him with a woman who was also closed off meant they both needed to grow and I'm happy they did.

They had many obstacles to overcome before they could have their happily-ever-after ending. Both had allowed the past to shape their present. Liz had to relinquish her need to always be the one helping and allow Blake and his team to help her rescue her sister. While Blake needed to learn to trust both Liz and God. Together they made a formidable team.

I'm busy now writing my next book that will be released in April 2016. The first in a new continuities series from Love Inspired Suspense set in a fictional town in Arizona and revolving around the training center of a Rookie K-9 Unit. My heroine trains puppies to be placed with officers. What could be cuter than puppies!

Blessings to you and yours,

LARGER-PRINT BOOKS!

GET 2 FREE
LARGER-PRINT NOVELS
PLUS 2 FREE
MYSTERY GIFTS

Love Inspired®

Larger-print novels are now available...

REQUEST YOUR FREE BOOKS!
2 FREE WHOLESOME ROMANCE NOVELS
IN LARGER PRINT
PLUS 2
FREE
MYSTERY GIFTS

⁂⁂⁂⁂⁂⁂⁂⁂⁂⁂⁂⁂⁂⁂⁂⁂⁂⁂⁂⁂

HEARTWARMING™

⁂⁂⁂⁂⁂⁂⁂⁂⁂⁂⁂⁂⁂⁂⁂⁂⁂⁂⁂⁂

Wholesome, tender romances

YES! Please send me 2 FREE Harlequin® Heartwarming Larger-Print novels and my 2 FREE mystery gifts (gifts worth about $10). After receiving them, if I don't wish to receive any more books, I can return the shipping statement marked "cancel." If I don't cancel, I will receive 4 brand-new larger-print novels every month and be billed just $5.24 per book in the U.S. or $5.99 per book in Canada. That's a savings of at least 19% off the cover price. It's quite a bargain! Shipping and handling is just 50¢ per book in the U.S. and 75¢ per book in Canada.* I understand that accepting the 2 free books and gifts places me under no obligation to buy anything. I can always return a shipment and cancel at any time. Even if I never buy another book, the two free books and gifts are mine to keep forever.

161/361 IDN GHX2

Name _____ (PLEASE PRINT) _____

Address _____ Apt. # _____

City _____ State/Prov. _____ Zip/Postal Code _____

Signature (if under 18, a parent or guardian must sign) _____

Mail to the **Reader Service:**
IN U.S.A.: P.O. Box 1867, Buffalo, NY 14240-1867
IN CANADA: P.O. Box 609, Fort Erie, Ontario L2A 5X3

* Terms and prices subject to change without notice. Prices do not include applicable taxes. Sales tax applicable in N.Y. Canadian residents will be charged applicable taxes. Offer not valid in Quebec. This offer is limited to one order per household. Not valid for current subscribers to Harlequin Heartwarming larger-print books. All orders subject to credit approval. Credit or debit balances in a customer's account(s) may be offset by any other outstanding balance owed by or to the customer. Please allow 4 to 6 weeks for delivery. Offer available while quantities last.

Your Privacy—The Reader Service is committed to protecting your privacy. Our Privacy Policy is available online at www.ReaderService.com or upon request from the Reader Service.

We make a portion of our mailing list available to reputable third parties that offer products we believe may interest you. If you prefer that we not exchange your name with third parties, or if you wish to clarify or modify your communication preferences, please visit us at www.ReaderService.com/consumerchoice or write to us at Reader Service Preference Service, P.O. Box 9062, Buffalo, NY 14240-9062. Include your complete name and address.

HW15

YES! Please send me **The Montana Mavericks Collection** in Larger Print. This collection begins with 3 FREE books and 2 FREE gifts (gifts valued at approx. $20.00 retail) in the first shipment, along with the other first 4 books from the collection! If I do not cancel, I will receive 8 monthly shipments until I have the entire 51-book Montana Mavericks collection. I will receive 2 or 3 FREE books in each shipment and I will pay just $4.99 US/ $5.89 CDN for each of the other four books in each shipment, plus $2.99 for shipping and handling per shipment.*If I decide to keep the entire collection, I'll have paid for only 32 books, because 19 books are FREE! I understand that accepting the 3 free books and gifts places me under no obligation to buy anything. I can always return a shipment and cancel at any time. My free books and gifts are mine to keep no matter what I decide.

263 HCN 2404 463 HCN 2404

Name	(PLEASE PRINT)	
Address		Apt. #
City	State/Prov.	Zip/Postal Code

Signature (if under 18, a parent or guardian must sign)

Mail to the **Reader Service**:

IN U.S.A.: P.O. Box 1867, Buffalo, NY 14240-1867
IN CANADA: P.O. Box 609, Fort Erie, Ontario L2A 5X3

MMLPBPA15

READERSERVICE.COM

Manage your account online!
- Review your order history
- Manage your payments
- Update your address

> ### We've designed the Reader Service website just for you.

Enjoy all the features!
- Discover new series available to you, and read excerpts from any series.
- Respond to mailings and special monthly offers.
- Connect with favorite authors at the blog.
- Browse the Bonus Bucks catalog and online-only exculsives.
- Share your feedback.

DISCARD

Visit us at:

ReaderService.com